The Tomcat's lock-on buzzer began blaring.

"We're locked-up," shouted the RIO. "Going to evasive." A string of magnesium flares shot from the underside of the Tomcat as it bat-turned into the target. To escape a heat-seeking missile, the best plan was electronic counter measures, flares or chaff, then turn inside, toward the missile, shielding the air-craft's engine's heat signature.

"Where's the missile?" the RIO wondered aloud.

The answer was swift and definitive. A strange, eerie, iridescent glow appeared as a long streak flashed on the radar scope, joining the target to the nose of the Tomcat.

Moments later, the Tomcat disintegrated. It had been shot down by a weapons system never before encountered by American fighter pilots.

Also by Tom Willard

Strike Fighters
Bold Forager
War Chariot
Sudden Fury
Red Dancer
Desert Star

Published by
<small>HARPERPAPERBACKS</small>

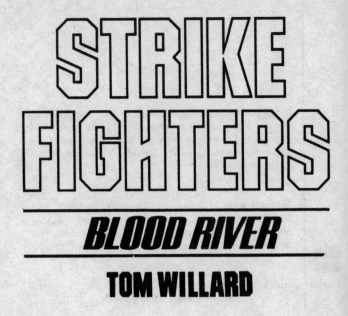

STRIKE FIGHTERS

BLOOD RIVER

TOM WILLARD

HarperPaperbacks
A Division of HarperCollins*Publishers*

This is a work of fiction. The characters, incidents, and dialogues are products of the author's imagination and are not to be construed as real. Any resemblance to actual events or persons, living or dead, is entirely coincidental.

HarperPaperbacks *A Division of* HarperCollins*Publishers*
10 East 53rd Street, New York, N.Y. 10022

Cover illustration by Attila Hejja

First printing: September 1991

Printed in the United States of America

HarperPaperbacks and colophon are trademarks of HarperCollins*Publishers*

10 9 8 7 6 5 4 3 2 1

For my mother and father, Faye and Norman Smith.

And to the memory of U.S. Navy F/A-18 Hornet "strike fighter" pilot Lt. Commander Michael S. Speicher, 33, USS *Saratoga*, the first American casualty in *Operation Desert Storm*.

Prologue

Baikanor. Soviet Union.

THE MORNING SUN ROSE ABOVE THE BLACKNESS OF southern Russia, turning the morning purple, then red, until the sky was gold. When the sky turned white, the new day had begun. Fresh. Clear. A perfect beginning for a day in the life of Major Yuri Demlov.

A day that would have to continue perfect—in every way—if the pilot was to see the sun rise again. That is, the sunrise over Baikanor.

Before his working day would end Demlov was scheduled to see the sun rise many times—from various points of the earth where he would be flying from the darkness of the east.

Chasing the sun.

Chasing the sun over the Indian Ocean. The Atlantic. The North American continent. The Pacific. Where he would begin the western glide slope back to Baikanor.

In the cockpit of the stealth fighter dubbed *Wolfhound* by the scientists and generals of the Soviet air force, Demlov adjusted the throttle settings and watched the multitude of computerized gauges react on the instrument panel as the planform cockpit rose above the wing-shaped fighter.

"Power coming up," Demlov reported calmly to the flight center at the Soviets' primary missile-testing complex.

Two Tumansky ramjet turbines began winding up and Demlov felt the titanium skin of the Wolfhound shiver as over one hundred thousand pounds of afterburning thrust began to awake.

The aircraft looked similar in design to the F-117A stealth fighter built at the Skunk Works in the United States.

But, unlike the F-117A, this aircraft carried sharp teeth, and had a capability no other aircraft had in the world: supersonic speed and a weapons system unheard of in the world.

"Clear for takeoff, Wolfhound," replied the director of the flight center, a Soviet scientist who had been involved in the project since 1986.

Demlov eased forward on the control stick and the huge bat-shaped fighter airplane responded smoothly, turning onto the long runway.

Demlov pressed a button marked SYSTEMS CHECK, and waited for the computer to check all the systems. A check that took the computer seconds. A check that would have taken Demlov several minutes to complete manually.

Seconds later he reported, "Power increasing."

The Wolfhound rolled along the concrete runway. A high-pitched howl whistled where the aircraft had been moments before, like a sewing machine running on full speed. Out of control.

But Demlov was in control. Control was not by arm

movement, nor hand movement. Control on the directional stick was more pulse sensation. A slight, imperceptible lean forward, or to the side for horizontal and longitudinal reaction.

"Rotation," Demlov reported moments later.

The sleek aircraft lifted off the runway.

The sky was still. There wasn't a sound as the aircraft's nose came up.

On the ground, there was nothing for the guards and other personnel to do except watch. Watch for a mere four seconds as the aircraft grew small, then smaller. Finally, it was no longer visible.

Wolfhound, the Soviet aircraft designed to avoid radar detection and deliver a horrifying weapon, had begun its first flight outside the Soviet Union with no more ceremony than the rising of the sun.

Hoedspruit. South Africa. 0530.

COLONEL COOS VAN MUERWE PULLED HIS SHORT, muscular frame from behind the wheel of his army jeep and marched briskly past two guards posted in front of the Strike Command headquarters building of the Suid-Afrikaanse Lugmag's No. 1 Squadron. The squadron, equipped with Dassault Mirage III strike/attack fighter/bombers, was considered one of the finest in the world. Van Muerwe, the squadron commander, had led the squadron in Angola and Namibia.

Van Muerwe was a legend in both the air—for his fighting skill and leadership—and on the ground, most notably for his staunch belief in the "cause."

Afrikaner.

He had deep, penetrating blue eyes and blond hair framing a sun-bronzed face that rarely showed emotion. The descendant of Boer *voetrekkers*, pioneers who ventured north from safety into the bush of Africa in 1838, van Muerwe was now standing at the center of the debate that would, in his opinion, destroy his country and bring political and economic collapse to the entire African continent.

He would not allow that, he thought while marching into the communications center in the headquarters building. A young officer was on duty. Standing, the young officer saluted and pointed at the bank of radio transmitters and receivers lining the wall.

They spoke in Afrikaans.

"Are the frequencies correct?" Muerwe asked while checking his watch.

"Ready to transmit, Colonel."

Van Muerwe sat at the transmitter and took a microphone. Studying his watch, he saw the seconds tick off until the minute hand reached 0545. At that precise moment, Colonel Coos van Muerwe keyed the microphone and spoke clearly.

"White lions."

One hundred twenty thousand feet above the Indian Ocean, Major Yuri Demlov was nearly outside the gravitational pull of the earth. The moon appeared larger than he ever imagined. The stars were near enough to touch. He had refueled over Egypt, then shot southwest, testing the surveillance of outer space satellites and ground-based radar systems of the United States overseeing the theater of operations in the Persian Gulf.

He was not afraid, but he did stiffen with anticipation when he heard the voice say, *"White lions!"*

Demlov quickly shut down all frequencies linking the Wolfhound with Baikanor.

Demlov then pushed the nose over, toward earth. Specifically, to a point that would allow him to set up the aircraft on a glide slope for a point he could not see— but knew was there—off the port wing.

At the flight center in Baikanor, the breathing had almost stopped completely as the Soviet scientists stared incredulously at the electronic world map where minutes before the signature of Wolfhound had burned brightly.

There was now no such signature.

"My God," said one scientist. "Where is the Wolfhound?"

Cruising at Angels fourteen—fourteen thousand feet— above the Indian Ocean, Navy Commander Lyle Bieswinger switched on the forward-looking infrared radar to FLIR-scan the ocean. On his vertical display indicator, an island came into view. The bearing was off the nose of the Tomcat. Since the Maldives lay behind his course, and the southwest coast of Africa lay off his starboard wing, he knew it could only be one island.

"Seychelles off our twelve o'clock position," Bieswinger reported to his RIO, the young radar intercept officer riding in the backseat of his F-14 Tomcat.

"Roger. Flight plan calls for us to gyro at Seychelles and return to Home Plate."

The RIO, Lt. j.g. Paul Shoemaker, was a new RIO fresh from Pawtuxent Naval Air Station. It was his first cruise since graduating from the naval academy. He was young, handsome, and eager to learn from the squadron commander, who generally took his new men up for their first ride after reporting aboard.

Home Plate was the designation for the nuclear aircraft carrier CVN 85 USS *Valiant*, a state-of-the-art weapons platform making for the Arabian Sea.

The carrier was six hundred miles away, off the coast of Oman. Part of a sixteen-ship battle group designated Zulu Station, the BG was assigned the task of guarding the southern entrance to the Persian Gulf.

The thought of so much sea duty often made Bieswinger wonder how he fathered four children, all the spitting image of the old man, erasing any thoughts of "back door" activity while on cruise. Must have been firing heat-seekers at the right biological moment, he always told himself with a satisfying grin. The same grin he was wearing behind the visor of his helmet.

This was it. His last flight before retirement. Time to put the Tomcat squadron in young, but capable hands and find that stretch of Wyoming grazing pasture he'd thought about for the past five years.

But first, there was business.

Bieswinger was reaching the point in the flight plan where it was time to swing back toward the BG. Fuel was ample. He could go to afterburner if necessary, but would need to tank from one of the KA-6 Intruders flying tanker duty if he thought there might be engagement.

Not tonight, he told himself. The F-14, the long-range punch for the carrier's protective cocoon, was carrying a variety of missiles: AIM-7 Sparrows, radar-guided ass-kickers; AIM-9L Sidewinders, close-in heat-seekers; and a Vulcan 20mm cannon for "pitcher's mound" activity. Close in. The fighter pilot's preference.

But the real role of the Tomcat came in the form

of the AIM-54 Phoenix missile. With a range of over one hundred miles, and a cost of a million dollars a shot, the Phoenix protected the carrier from incoming cruise missiles.

To kill the carrier the enemy had to first get past the Phoenix.

The Tomcat was the hunter at the leading edge. To get to the carrier, the enemy had to run a gauntlet of F-14s backed by an internally set protection cover from two squadrons of the new "tits machine"—the F/A-18 Hornet, the McDonnell-Douglas Strike/Fighter.

But first the enemy had to get past the F-14.

Bieswinger was preparing to go to full swept-wing for a 180-degree bat-turn when he heard the kid in the rear seat gasp.

"Jesus Christ! What is that!" Shoemaker's eyes were on the radar screen. A radar contact was moving across the screen at a rate that seemed impossible.

No transponder code. No IFF ident. Just a moving blur.

"Meteor?" Bieswinger answered, not certain.

"Too low. And the trajectory's all wrong. Besides, a meteor would have burned up by now on entry into the atmosphere," the RIO replied.

"You're not talking UFO, are you, son? That's a ton of paperwork," cautioned Bieswinger.

"I don't know what it is, Skipper. But it's nothing kin to the world we know."

"Better scope it out." Bieswinger sighed as he checked his fuel gauge. "We have a little fuel we can play around with. Not much."

The Tomcat lurched, then thundered through the sky when the pilot shoved the throttles through military power to Zone Five afterburner.

Seconds later the RIO whispered, "The target is pulling away." There was a pause, then, "My God . . . that sucker's doing at least Mach four."

There was a momentary silence, then Bieswinger's stomach tightened and he knew the target was not a meteor.

"What the hell!" shouted Shoemaker.

"Target turning," said Bieswinger while depressing the commo button and reported, "Home Plate, this is Coyote pack leader. Have unidentified target turning onto my twelve." Bieswinger's eyes widened in astonishment as the target shot past his canopy, then swung onto his tail. "Negative. Gomer now on my six. Right on my tail."

Before the reply from the carrier could be heard, the sound of the lock-on buzzer began blaring.

"We're locked up," shouted the RIO. "Going to evasive." A string of magnesium flares shot from the underside of the Tomcat, appearing like a string of burning pearls as the Tomcat bat-turned into the target. To escape a heat-seeking missile, the best plan was electronic countermeasures, flares or chaff, then turn inside, toward the missile, shielding the aircraft's engine heat signature, the source of the homing missile.

"Where's the missile!" the RIO wondered. "Where's the fucking missile!"

The answer came as the pilots were trapped in a cloud of confusion. An answer swift and definitive.

There was the buzzing of the lock-up, and then a strange, eerie, iridescent glow. A long streak appeared on the radar scope, joining the target to the nose of the Tomcat.

Outside, the blackness turned to brilliant light. Bieswinger thought he was caught in a shaft of lightning. The cockpit turned green-white for a second. There was the sensation of heat. His body felt as though it were aflame. The instrument panel was smoking. He thought he was blind. He went for the last resort. The ejection handle above his head.

"Eject! Eject! Eject!" ordered Bieswinger. Standard ejection procedure was set in motion by the first call of "eject," meaning get ready for the "loud exit." The second "eject" meant the rear seat was already starting the rocket-sled ride upward. The front seat would go on the third "eject."

The moment the canopy blew off, the Tomcat disintegrated. The MK-GRU7A ejection seats' rockets were in the process of firing when the fuselage melted, then the swept wings, finally the tail section.

Somewhere in the middle of the meltdown, Bieswinger and Shoemaker lost control of their SA—situational awareness—and, more importantly, contact with life.

At Hoedspruit, Colonel Coos van Muerwe was climbing into a helo when the voice of the young officer at the squadron headquarters crackled over the communications headset.

"The aircraft is inbound for landing. There was one minor problem, however."

"What problem?" Van Muerwe demanded.

"Contact with an aircraft."

Van Muerwe thought to swear, then relaxed. A smile cut across his tough features.

"What was the aircraft's nationality?"

"American."

"Was a distress signal transmitted?"

"No, sir," replied the commo officer.

Van Muerwe nodded sharply. "Good. Then we are safe." He increased the throttle, hauled back on the cyclic, and lifted the Alouette into the black sky.

Speeding east, toward another rendezvous, he smiled, knowing that he was flying toward a new South Africa.

A South Africa the White Lions would die—and kill—for in order to have a homeland for the Afrikaner!

PART ONE: RETIEF'S VISION

0715. Indian Ocean.

BOULTON SACRETTE WAS A CAPTAIN IN THE UNITED States Navy. He was also the CAG, the commander of the air wing, which meant he was responsible for the lives of several thousand men serving the nuclear aircraft carrier USS *Valiant*, the core of the navy's rapid deployment battle group designated Zulu Station.

Right now he felt like a father who had lost a son. Two sons, to be precise. Lost forever to the deep of the Indian Ocean.

At forty-three, Sacrette had more combat flying time than any active duty navy fighter jock. Death was no stranger. Losing friends came with the job. That was a reality he had lived with for over twenty years.

But that didn't make the loss any goddamned easier to take. Not by a long shot.

A fighter pilot never forgets that their number can turn without notice, whether in a shooting war, a night carrier landing, or a disastrous catapult launch.

Death came with the territory. Every working day. Every working moment. And with the death there was the human factor: the need to reevaluate one's place. The job. The risk. It was human. It was natural. Which was why Sacrette was the CAG. He could be wild, unruly, even unpredictable. But he was, above all else, naturally human. Instinctive. Calculating. Reckless at times, but not unnecessarily reckless, a characteristic he recognized in himself while watching for the same in his men.

Unnecessarily reckless. The words echoed through his mind as he thought about Bieswinger. Shoemaker. One was certainly not. The other hadn't had enough time to learn.

Sacrette was tall, wiry, with dark hair and deep cerulean eyes. His square jaw was from his French-Canadian ancestry. Ancestry that had proved its durability from the Hudson Bay Company of the eighteenth century to the Montana ranchers of the twentieth century.

A heritage he walked away from at eighteen to attend the U.S. Naval Academy.

Sacrette wanted to fly fighter planes, not become a rancher.

Sacrette wanted to lead men through the sky into battle, not cattle over a cattle guard to pasture.

He still was certain of that, even while thinking of the two dead aviators.

That was when something caught his eye.

"Switch on the elevator, son. I want a closer inspection." Sacrette ordered the sailor operating the hoist in the SH-60 Seahawk. He pointed to wreckage floating on the surface thirty feet below. The pilot hovered while Sacrette slipped a bridle around his waist, then leaned out. The electrical whirr of the winch grew softer as Sacrette neared the surface.

Motioning to halt, Sacrette was nearly touching the water as he reached and touched a piece of debris that was once part of the fuselage. The radome, where the AWG-9 radar was housed on the nose cone, was absent. A black, charred hole had been burned through the nose to the firewall of the forward cockpit area. A part of the cockpit was still intact, except for the canopy and the seats.

On the fuselage the name of the pilot was still visible, though badly scorched.

Commander Lyle Bieswinger.

Sacrette patted the name, then ran his hand along the metal to the edge of the piece of aircraft.

Suspicion clouded his face; he knew there was something about the texture of the metal where the jagged edges caused by impact appeared different.

Smooth. Not sharp and razorlike. Smooth.

The plane wasn't torn apart on impact. It was torn apart before impact he thought. And there was only one way that could happen: It had to have been shot down!

But there was more confusion. He had seen a lot of aircraft wreckage. The edges of the metal should still be sharp, not smooth. The Tomcat's metal edges were beaded, as though welded, or brazed by extreme heat.

Glancing up, he could see in the distance the nuclear-powered guided-missile cruiser USS *California* approaching the helo's position. Sacrette gave a thumbs-up to the winch operator and was drawn into the hull of the helo.

Slipping into the webbed seat braced to the bulkhead, Sacrette grew quiet. Sullen. The anger was coursing through his system. He hated losing men. It was loathsome.

Then a strange question formed in his mind: *How many had he seen die?*

The men from Viet Nam he recalled with ease, they were his friends. His brothers. Men he ate with. Chased women with. Fought with and fought beside. His brother pilots. They weren't his buddies. They were his family.

Since Nam all that had changed. Staying in the navy and wearing the gold wings of a naval aviator he had progressed up the ladder of rank, as did the others who had survived and stayed in the service. Three tours as squadron exec aboard three different carriers. Then his first tour as squadron commander. Then another.

With the assumption of command came the distinction between him and the pilots. A distinction he slowly recognized, and slowly accepted. The change in role brought new responsibilities; new pilots. *Young* pilots.

He couldn't go carousing with them in Barcelona or San Diego, or sneak women aboard in his duffel bags, like the stripper that had danced on the ejection seat of an F-4 for the squadron in the hangar deck that warm night in Lisbon. He had to set an example. He had to make the decisions and with each decision he found himself moving further from the center of the greatest excitement he had ever known: the camaraderie of the greatest pilots in the world.

"Do you want me to continue the search, Thunderbolt?" The voice of the helo pilot was barely audible through the roar of the massive helo's rotor slap. He was obviously willing to continue the search despite the fact that it was hopeless.

Sacrette shook his head, then turned back to the sea.

The *California* would recover the wreckage, what there was to recover, then transport the remnants to the *Valiant* for further investigation.

There the tedious task of solving the mystery would begin. A mystery Sacrette was already mulling over in his mind. A mystery he knew would lead to the conclusion he had already drawn: The Tomcat had been shot down by a weapons system never before encountered by American fighter pilots.

2

THE WRECKAGE FROM THE F-14 TOMCAT WAS SPREAD along an area of the USS *Valiant* hangar deck specifically selected as the reassembly location. What wreckage there was. Part of the fuselage. A piece of the starboard wing.

"What about the bodies?" Admiral Elrod Lord asked Sacrette, who was kneeling over the piece of fuselage he had discovered earlier that morning.

Lord was a square-shouldered no-nonsense commander who stood slightly shorter than Sacrette. Their relationship stemmed from the Viet Nam war, when Sacrette, a fresh j.g. from flight school, stormed aboard the *Kitty Hawk*, where Lord was the CAG.

"What in the hell is that critter?" Lord had asked Sacrette incredulously, staring at a chimpanzee that was perched on Sacrette's shoulder.

A young, fiery-eyed Boulton Sacrette replied, "My RIO. His name's Martini. He's a good hand, except when he pisses on my helmet."

Nearly thirty years later, the wreckage before him now reminded Lord again of Martini. The chimp was lost over the Red River valley of North Viet Nam when Sacrette was shot down in his F-4 Phantom.

"I repeat, Captain . . . What about the bodies?"

Sacrette shook his head. "Air Sea Rescue reported they found nothing. It's logical to conclude that the bodies will not be recovered."

Lord didn't look surprised; recovery in the ocean was always near impossible. "What do you suspect was the cause of this crash, Captain?"

Sacrette shook his head. "You won't like what you're going to hear."

"I'll be the judge of that. Say what's on your mind."

Sacrette ran his hand along the edge of the metal near Bieswinger's name. "The aircraft was shot down."

"Impossible," Lord replied emphatically. "Had the aircraft been in an engagement Bieswinger would have been in communication with the CIC. There was no communication."

Sacrette shook his head. "Not if the Tomcat's radar and communications were destroyed."

Lord's eyebrows raised slightly above his gray eyes. "Meaning what? There's no such weapon capability that I'm aware of. At least, not outside of theory."

"Meaning . . ." Sacrette paused momentarily, then shrugged and rubbed his hands tightly as he stood facing the battle group commander. "There may be such a weapon available now. I think Lyle was hit by something so devastating he didn't have time to contact the *Valiant*, much less engage the attacker. Something so devastating it literally melted the radar and commo systems in his aircraft. With the crew blind—and out of commo link— they were helpless."

"Get to the point, Captain."

Sacrette sighed. "A beam weapon. A particle beam weapon designed to destroy radio frequencies, radar, and blind both the electro-optical sights and the air crew."

Lord looked incredulously at Sacrette. "You mean a laser?"

"Yes, sir. A laser."

Admiral Lord released a long sigh. "Jesus." He thought for a moment. "Could the Iraqis have such a weapon?"

Sacrette shook his head. "No way. There's only one country I know of that could have such a weapon without our knowledge."

"The Soviet Union," Lord said flatly. Then, as quickly, "The Russians wouldn't dare pull this kind of stunt."

Sacrette laughed sarcastically. "What better way to test the theory than under the cover of a desert patrol? Refueling wouldn't be that difficult, not for the Sovs, who patrol this area on a regular basis. They have long-range refueling aircraft from Viet Nam, Mozambique, and Zimbabwe."

Sacrette was referring to the continuing U.N. operation directed at the Iraq military threat in the Persian Gulf. An operation the battle group was steaming toward at flank speed to take up the southern patrol arena in the Gulf of Oman at the mouth of the Strait of Hormuz.

Sacrette was delighted that the day was approaching when the talking would stop and the business of war begin, as far as his battle group was concerned.

Hussein was a piss-ant in Sacrette's eyes. A cowardly madman who had invaded and usurped a neighboring nation, committed acts of atrocities, and was attempting to expand the threat of world war by developing chemical and nuclear weapons. To stop Hussein, one-half million allied fighting troops stood on the other side of the line drawn in the Saudi Arabian sand.

"If not the Soviets," Lord said, thinking aloud, "who? The only other country that might have that technology in this area is South Africa. I can't imagine the South Africans firing on an American aircraft without provocation."

Sacrette had no idea. Before he could say another word a voice came over the intercom. "Admiral Lord. Report to the bridge. Message from J.C."

Sacrette recognized the call sign of the Joint Chiefs. The two men saluted; Sacrette went back to pondering the fate of the F-14. Lord hurried to the bridge.

In the CIC, Lord took the red telephone linking him through satellite to the Chief of Naval Operations, the senior naval officer on the Joint Chiefs of Staff.

He listened while the CNO explained a developing situation. Lord checked his watch and nodded as though the CNO was watching his response. "We'll get under way immediately, sir," Lord said in reply.

Hanging up the telephone, Lord took the carrier's internal MC-1 microphone and ordered, "Captain Sacrette, assemble VFA-101 in the ready room, immediately."

Throughout the carrier a pulsation began throbbing through the crew of sixty-five hundred.

A pulsation that the men had come to recognize whenever there was something about to happen.

When a hunt was about to begin.

3

THE READY ROOM OF THE VFA-101 FIGHTING HORNETS rocked with anticipation, and the eyes of the jet jocks there beamed that special look of men who knew that their special skills might soon be in demand.

Sacrette sat beside Lieutenants Ryan "Rhino" Michaels, Sean "Gooze" Thomas, and Brent "Gompers" Stevens. Three of his best—and most daring—young pilots. The younger pilots kept looking around; Sacrette appeared ready to fall asleep. It had been a long morning. Besides, he had sat through too many scuttlebutt calls not to know that each order to the ready room didn't necessarily signal a call to arms.

The admiral probably wanted to discuss flight ops as the carrier began its run toward the Gulf of Oman in preparation to setting up their patrol sector in the southern end of the area of operation.

Or so he thought. His thoughts changed when Lord entered and marched sharply toward the podium.

Lord switched on a television that depicted a map overview of the Horn of Africa, as the area on the easternmost part of Africa was known.

A close-up revealed the small country of Somalia, a desert country the size of Texas.

Lord tapped the screen. "Gentlemen," then he nodded at Commander Laura "Jugs" Wagner, the VFA-101 exec and only female on the carrier. "And lady. We have a developing situation. The Chief of Naval Ops wants the battle group to alter course and move toward the east coast of Somalia. As you may know, there has been civil war in Somalia for several years. It appears the insurgents are gaining the upper hand over the situation. The Somalia President, Mohammed Siad Barre, has requested military assistance from the United States and Italy. The rebels, Sunni Moslems who call themselves the United Sunni Congress, have taken Mogadishu, the capital."

A low grumble threaded through the gathering of pilots. It seemed the entire Moslem world was rapidly approaching war. Iraq. Kuwait. Saudi Arabia. Now Somalia. Though still African, Somalis considered themselves to be Arabs.

"What about American personnel?" Sacrette asked. He knew two American pilots were assigned to the prowestern air force as advisers.

"The diplomatic personnel are currently holed up in the American embassy. And they have company."

"What company?" Jugs asked.

Lord grinned quickly, then grew serious. "The Soviet ambassador and his staff are currently receiving diplomatic shelter in the American embassy."

Laughter rolled through the ready room.

"What exactly is the *Valiant*'s mission?" asked Sacrette.

"This operation is to merely assist in the peaceful withdrawal of Americans—and friends—from the capital. We are not to engage in hostilities. I repeat: *not* to engage in hostilities with the rebels. A heliborne force will fly marines to the embassy from one of our amphibious carriers. The heloes will make the extraction of diplomatic personnel and withdraw immediately."

"What about rebel ground fire?" asked Sacrette.

"The rebel forces have assured our embassy personnel there will be no harassment from either ground fire or aircraft." Lord's comment was accompanied by a look of doubt. Then he added a footnote: "But I believe it prudent to assume the rebels have now taken the air base and possibly have pilots willing to fly for the rebels."

"I've heard that before," Sacrette replied acidly. "I recommend we back up the heloes with ready-to-launch air and strike cover."

Lord nodded his approval. "Have air and strike aircraft in Alert Five. Should there be trouble, we'll be ready. Questions?"

There were none. Lord left and Sacrette finalized the flight end of the operations with Jugs and the other pilots.

Some would sit at Alert Five, buckled and locked into the catapult; the remainder would sit in their aircraft on the flight deck. The Alert Five would provide an instantaneous air and strike response composed of two aircraft in each mode. The remaining strike/fighters would be on the flight deck waiting to follow the Alert Five, should trouble develop.

4

SACRETTE WENT TO HIS QUARTERS WHERE HE TOOK the time to complete one final duty before dressing and climbing into his aircraft. He took out his writing materials and wrote brief letters to the wife of Bieswinger and the parents of Shoemaker. He didn't know the younger pilot as well as Bieswinger, but he knew the breed. The courage. The loyalty to crew and country.

The letters were difficult to write. It was another prerequisite of command, one he had learned from Admiral Lord, who once advised him: "If writing these letters ever becomes easy . . . it's time for you to go back to Montana."

The letters were still difficult. He sealed both letters and dropped them into the mail pouch near the carrier's snack bar and then went to his locker.

Ten minutes later the CAG was climbing into the cockpit, and the question was still gnawing at him: Who could have shot down the F-14?

"Alright, Thunderbolt, get your head into the business at hand," he reminded himself. Sitting in the cockpit, he attached the lugs of the seat pack to his torso harness, attached the inflater hose to his "speed jeans," the inflatable pants that fought the effects of high g-stress, then connected his parachute riser lugs to the capewells on his harness.

A brown-shirted sailor, called a plane captain, connected the nose gear to a motorized cart that guided the Hornet to one of the electrical elevators. There was a loud whirring electrical sound as the platform rode into the clear sky of the flight deck.

Within minutes he was locked into the tension of the catapult, then he sat back and did what he had done thousands of times: He waited to be launched into the fury of war.

1800. Moscow.

IN THE SOVIET UNION, THE SKY WAS DARK. INTO THE darkness Major Viktor Tragor hurried down the steps of his apartment off Kalunin Square; the click of his highly polished boots sounded with the same urgency as the telephone call he had received less than an hour before.

The telephone call had set off an immediate warning in his brain; a warning that all KGB officers innately acquired over the years of service.

A summons generally meant trouble, or a new assignment. Tragor had festered in his apartment for nearly eight months since his return from South Africa. New assignment? Why? His last assignment had ended unsuccessfully, ripping him from the inner circle of the KGB to the dreariness of banishment.

Bounding to the sidewalk, he paused to look around. Perhaps, he thought, for the last time. The thought didn't seem to bother him. Anything was better than what he had endured over the last eight months.

The sky was hazy; the taste of the air putrid from the acrid smell of pollution caused by nearby factories.

Old women moved methodically along the streets sweeping with their dirt-stained swish brooms. Their faces were devoid of smiles; their eyes vacant.

At the curb, a black *zil* waited, the rear door held open by a young lieutenant; a red, hurried shave burned the young officer's face. He stared-straight ahead as Tragor entered the car.

Tragor paused as he slid into the seat. His features immediately registered surprise when he saw a man seated inside, watching the KGB officer.

"Good afternoon, Comrade General." Tragor's voice was steady, but cautious. It wasn't every day that he was invited to ride with the chairman of the KGB's First Directorate.

Major General Pietor Borynov reclined against the rear seat. His dark eyes roved over the younger officer as though he were searching for something particular. After a strained pause, he nodded for Tragor to be seated.

Borynov came directly to the point. "You are most fortunate, Major Tragor. It appears your long absence from the First Directorate may be over."

Tragor couldn't hide his approval. "I would be most grateful for the opportunity to return to service, Comrade General."

"I make no promises. The decision lies with other authority."

Tragor skewed his head sideways and tried to interpret the chairman's meaning. *Other authority?*

Borynov chuckled and appeared pleased with putting the bug in Tragor's mind.

"You will be surprised," he added. "Of that you can be certain."

Nothing more was said. The *zil* sped north along

Leningratsky Prospekt, out of the capital, into the wooded countryside. At a gravel road the *zil* turned off where a sign warned: **Halt! Conservation Area**.

Tragor laughed to himself. Then he grew more interested at what he saw on the road. The half-mile drive to the main gate, where a sergeant directed the automobile to a parking lot, was lined with KGB soldiers of the Border Guard Directorate, spaced at thirty-meter intervals.

In the parking lot he studied the cars parked in the special parking lot, which was surrounded by a chain-linked fence topped with ribbon wire. The razor-edged wire gleamed eerily in the night, as insidious as most of the men who passed through the gates.

Except, possibly, for one of those men. Which made him understand the need for the increased security. A Mercedes-Benz gleamed in the sunlight. The Mercedes, a gift from the Swiss ambassador, was the personal car of the General Secretary of the Soviet Union. Sitting beside the Mercedes was another prominent vehicle, a Fiat, owned by the Chairman General of the KGB.

Tragor knew instinctively that his life was about to change dramatically.

Another cold reality struck his mind: *This time, there would be no room for failure.*

6

THE FIRST DIRECTORATE HEADQUARTERS WAS A bronze building of Finnish design with lavish gardens concealing electronic mines, and laser sensors designed to detect body heat within a range of ninety to one hundred degrees Fahrenheit. This prevented the vicious komondor guard dogs roaming the fenced grounds from activating the sensors prematurely.

Following Borynov, Tragor marched briskly through the glass doors of the center, produced his KGB identity, and glanced around while the security officer checked his credentials.

In the foyer stood a bust of Felix Dzershinsky, the founder of the Cheka, the forerunner of the KGB. Off to one side was a restaurant where the best food in the Soviet Union could be found. A newspaper and tobacco kiosk was on the opposite side of the restaurant.

Tragor noticed that all the people in the building were smiling, unlike the peasants of Moscow.

The KGB took good care of its own.

"Major Tragor. Your clearance," said the security

officer. He handed Tragor a badge. The officer then punched several buttons on a computer keyboard, registering the identity number of the badge. A numbered signature appeared on the screen, the same number as on the badge. The officer then pressed the "delete" button, eliminating the number from the screen. Tragor understood.

The sensors in the building were designed to pick up body heat, except by those wearing the badges erased by the computer. An unauthorized person without a badge would be detected while a badge wearer would become invisible. Bodies detected were assumed to be in the building without authorization.

In essence, if a person was authorized to be in the building they simply did not exist.

Following Borynov, the two officers proceeded to an elevator, taking the short ride to the top floor, where the ultra-secret Zenith Room was located. The Zenith Room was the KGB code name for the communications center. There was a similar room in each Soviet embassy and consulate throughout the world.

Protected from satellite surveillance, the room offered the greatest privacy in the Soviet Union. The world, for that matter.

Seated around a long table were several men, including the General Secretary, the Chairman General of the KGB, the Supreme Soviet Air Marshal, and several members of the Politburo.

"Be seated." Gorbachev motioned to a chair at the end of the table.

Tragor seated himself somewhat nervously. His deep blue eyes glanced from one face to the next as he examined the most powerful men in the Soviet Union.

He didn't have to wonder if his presence was important; that was obvious. Nor did he wonder if he would accept whatever assignment would evolve from the meeting. He would accept whatever mission was offered.

He felt an enormous sense of relief. For a former elite intelligence officer to be banished from the world he loved was the worst punishment possible.

Not even the dank dungeons of the KGB's Lubyanka prison frightened him at this moment.

"Major Tragor," the General Secretary began slowly, "we have a matter of state security that requires the expertise of a man of your background."

"I will do whatever I'm requested to do, Comrade General Secretary."

The men at the table stiffened and Tragor thought he was finished before he began. It was no longer considered wise to refer to the General Secretary as "comrade."

Gorbachev smiled the polite, cold smile he was known for, then explained the situation involving the disappearance of the Wolfhound. When finished, he pointed to a computerized map on the wall. A series of red dots tracked the flight path of the Wolfhound, ending over the Indian Ocean.

"The Wolfhound flew over the Saudi Arabian desert to test the radar capabilities of the Americans posted since the invasion of Kuwait. Prior to refueling over the Indian Ocean, the aircraft disappeared from our radar screens."

Borynov asked, "What are your thoughts on the matter, Major?"

Tragor thought very carefully as he studied the flight path. There were several possibilities. "The aircraft could have developed engine trouble and crashed in the sea. That is my first reaction."

Borynov prodded further. "Do you have other thoughts, Major?"

Tragor could taste the innuendo. "But, of course, there is always the possibility of defection. In which case, there are numerable choices available to the pilot. Seychelles. Malagasy. Mozambique. Even Diego Garcia. The Americans have a naval facility on Diego Garcia."

Air Marshal Federovich spoke up: "We've considered the possibility of engine failure and loss at sea. The locator beacon used to transmit a downed aircraft's location was not activated."

"Is it possible that the aircraft's destruction was spontaneous?"

Federovich sneered as though he wanted to laugh at the absurdity of such a notion. "There was no debris noted on the satellite radar tracking the Wolfhound."

"Then I suggest the pilot flew to Diego Garcia. That's the likeliest location."

"The Wolfhound did not fly to Diego Garcia, and the other locations are excluded because we have intelligence operatives at the various airports capable of receiving the Wolfhound. Which leaves us with only one possibility. That possibility was confirmed by intercepted American communiques reporting the downing of an American F-14 fighter on patrol between Madagascar and Cape Town, South Africa."

Tragor understood. He had been the South African Resident for ten years for the Illegals Division of the First Directorate. Betrayal by one of his operatives compromised his identity, sending him scurrying for Mozambique, where he barely escaped the SA Special Branch.

The network was still in place, known only to Tragor and the chairman of the First Directorate. A replacement had not as yet been selected.

"That creates a new set of hazards we must risk in order to determine the location of the aircraft. Do you understand?"

Tragor understood. "I could be captured by the South Africans."

Gorbachev nodded. "We must have proof the South African government has possession of the Wolfhound. At which time we will deal with the de Klerk government."

"And if the government refuses to return the aircraft?" asked Tragor. He knew the answer before it was given.

"You are to destroy the Wolfhound. But first . . . the aircraft must be found!"

7

Nagmaal Farm. Natal Province.

SURROUNDED BY THE MAJESTIC DRAKENSBERG MOUNtains, Colonel Coos van Muerwe's farm sat in the heart of a vast, fertile valley in Natal Province. The farm, called *Nagmaal*, or "night communion" in Afrikaans, didn't look like a fortress. Not to the casual observer. Nor did the farm look like a place of holy communion.

It did, however, look like a place of communion. Military communion.

Closer inspection revealed farm hands harvesting crops under the protective eye of armed security guards patrolling the property with vicious attack dogs. Sandbagged machine-gun positions were set up along the perimeter of the main house where the gravel, circular driveway was lined with automobiles, jeeps, and three light battle tanks. Sitting atop the turret of each tank was a young white officer, scanning the outlying perimeter with a Bren heavy machine gun.

Behind the main house stood a barn. A road leading from the fields ended abruptly at the massive doors of the barn. Doors that were electronically controlled; doors guarded by more young men carrying automatic weapons.

Inside the barn, Coos van Muerwe was standing with a group of legislators who had arrived at noon from Pretoria. Each of the legislators was a proven loyalist to the Afrikaner movement. More important, they were members of White Lions, the right-wing political party born out of frustration with the government's stance on apartheid.

Jacob Shorn was a heavyset, balding farmer from the Transvaal. His thick, bushy eyebrows danced wildly above his fiery eyes as he listened to van Muerwe explain the newest piece of equipment enlisted into the movement.

"Gentlemen, this is the Wolfhound." As he motioned with his arm, several of van Muerwe's men removed a heavy tarp from the fighter.

The Wolfhound gleamed beneath the overhead lights; an ominous shape, it commanded the attention of those present.

Shorn released a long, sudden gasp, as though struck in the midsection. "It's magnificent, Colonel."

The others in the group walked toward the fighter, staring in awe at the sleek machine.

"Mein Gott," said Samuel Kroon, a rancher from Blomfontein, "I've never seen such an aircraft! Is it as awesome in application as it is in appearance?"

"It's likely you'll never see another of this type. And certainly, the capabilities of the Wolfhound are greater than one can imagine," van Muerwe boasted proudly.

"Where is the pilot?" asked another.

"He is in the command center."

"Bring him here. I wish to have him give us a critique on the aircraft," said Shorn.

Van Muerwe spoke into a small transmitter, and minutes later Major Yuri Demlov appeared. He was dressed in slacks and a short-sleeved shirt. He looked relaxed. He looked wealthy.

Which he was.

"How much did the aircraft cost, Colonel?" asked Shorn.

"Two million dollars," van Muerwe replied.

Shorn, the financial director of the White Lions, nearly choked.

Van Muerwe could see the consternation on Shorn's face, prompting him to add confidently, "Two million dollars well spent. This aircraft will provide us the blueprint to build a fleet of aircraft that can protect us from any aggressor. With this aircraft we have a weapon and delivery capability that will render an enemy air squadron helpless. Concurrently, the aircraft can be deployed at ground-based communications centers. This will eliminate the potential of collateral damage."

"What is collateral damage?" asked Kroon.

"Collateral damage is the civilian population manning the various centers. We are being very careful not to harm anyone unnecessarily. They are to be our allies—not our enemies."

"A wise decision, Colonel," said Kroon.

There was a continuing look of distress on the features of Shorn. "I still question whether the weapon is necessary. You are aware that at this point we are still conducting a dialogue with key members of the government. This great expense may not be necessary since we're not certain that the military option is necessary."

Van Muerwe nodded gracefully. "I believe time is running out for the political option. Nonetheless, we'll be prepared." Behind his eyes his thoughts were certain. The military option was the only option.

"What are the capabilities?" asked Kroon.

Van Muerwe motioned to Demlov, who stepped forward to explain. "The Wolfhound is a Mach five aircraft, capable of outrunning and outmaneuvering any conventional heat- or radar-seeking missile."

"What if the aircraft is boxed in? Couldn't an opposing aircraft lock on to the heat emission?" asked Shorn.

Demlov appeared amused at the question. "No. The radar's infrared sensors pick up heat emission—called a heat signature. Engine heat on conventional aircraft is projected from the engine exhaust nozzles in a concentrated exhaust emission. In the Wolfhound, the engine heat is evenly dispersed along the trailing edge of the wings. But first, a unique process occurs: the exhaust is air-cooled, emitting a cool exhaust, rather than hot exhaust. The next step is simple: The exhaust is vented through dozens of emitters. Quite frankly, I could turn on the engines and lower the temperature in this barn by fifteen degrees. It is, in essence, a giant flying air conditioner."

"Tell them about ground or airborne observation," said van Muerwe.

Demlov grinned. "There is a computer that allows the fabric of the aircraft to be 'painted' electronically to match the surrounding atmosphere. In blue sky, the belly of the aircraft is painted blue against a blue sky. The top of the aircraft can be painted to match the landscape below. In fact, if the Wolfhound is flown through a cloud, it can become the color of the cloud. Invisible to the enemy radar, or the pilot's natural vision, the Mark-one eyeball. The phrase used as the perfect pilot eyesight. Better than twenty-twenty vision."

"Incredible," gasped Shorn, who was now standing at the leading edge of the starboard wing.

"Another unique feature about Wolfhound," said van Muerwe, "is that unlike the American F-117A stealth fighter, this aircraft is a dogfighter. It can fly at slower airspeed, to retain the stealth capability and not leave a supersonic footprint; or it can go supersonic when necessary. The F-117A is slow in comparison to a fighter, or a bomber. More important, the F-117A uses conventional ordinance. The Wolfhound does not use bombs or rockets."

"What?" came the collective response.

Demlov patted a pod at the nose of the stealth fighter. "This is a particle beam projector. The beam— or laser—deactivates the opposing aircraft's radar and radio frequency weapons systems, while simultaneously destroying all electrical optical sighting devices. In effect, the opposing air crew becomes blind and helpless."

Van Muerwe's voice became severe. "In other words, gentlemen, the Wolfhound can destroy any opposing target—or radar installation—before the opponent can get off a shot. That has already been proven to me. I'm satisfied there is nothing that can prevent the Wolfhound from completing one of the most critical phases of Operation Lion's Laager."

Demlov rocked on his heels, then boasted, "I can destroy any plane—or pilot—in the world. There's no one who can stop me once we're in the air."

8

1700.

THE COAST OF SOMALIA APPEARED IN A HAZE TO THE west; waves of heat wafted off the waves, rising from the coast where the beach separating the turquoise sea from the sun-baked desert was a thin white line. Above, the sky was more white than blue.

"God Almighty," breathed CPO Desmond "Diamonds" Farnsworth. "It's hotter than a whore's breath."

As he looked up to the pilot reclining in his aircraft on the deck of the *Valiant*, sweat streamed down the face of the VFA-101 Fighting Hornets maintenance chief. His black skin was somewhat ashen; his shaved head gleamed.

Sacrette was sitting in the cockpit of his F/A-18D Hornet Strike/Fighter, wearing a *Top Gun* baseball hat to shade his eyes against the sun. He seemed lost in his thoughts, or simply ignoring the chief, which he often did when locked into Alert Five, buckled up and ready to launch from the bow catapult.

"Ain't you hot, Thunderbolt?" The chief seemed to be trying to push the conversation. Sacrette had said very little since the recovery of the F-14 Tomcat.

"Hot as a pistol, Chief. Too goddamm hot for conversation. So why don't you go to the maintenance crib and find something to do—or I'll find something for you to do. Like swab the decks of this carrier with a toothbrush!" Sacrette glared down at the chief. A glare Diamonds had seen on a thousand occasions; had ignored on a thousand occasions. Part of his job was to get through to the men who were hurting in the squadron.

Farnsworth laughed and ran his hand along the leading edge of the sleek F/A-18, the fleet's newest "tits machine." Painted in low-visibility gray, the Hornet was a multirole aircraft: a strike bomber or a fighter interceptor. Bad to the bone, was how the pilots referred to the Hornet.

"You've got to lighten up, Thunderbolt."

Sacrette shrugged, and hooded his cold blue cobra eyes against the haze wafting off the bow of the catapult. He had not stopped trying to solve the mystery of Bieswinger's death since he found the part of the forward fuselage. Questions kept surfacing. Answers lay in a void beyond his grasp. He knew one thing for certain: Bieswinger couldn't have been taken down that easily.

He was too damn *good*!

Farnsworth started to say something when he saw Sacrette stiffen in the cockpit. Suddenly he was removing his *Top Gun* hat and slipping on his helmet. Buckling the harness lugs of his torso harness to the seat, he quickly pulled down his helmet, raising the visor to examine the instrument panel.

"Clear the deck, Chief. The you-know-what's about to hit the Westinghouse."

Farnsworth didn't need to clarify. He had seen the Sacrette intuition at work before. The CAG could smell a fight. Farnsworth knew that look of the wolf in Sacrette's eyes. The look that said . . . "Another hunt is on!"

That's when the air boss's voice boomed from the pry-fly tower.

"Launch the Alert Five. Launch the Alert Five."

Minutes later, Sacrette was bringing the F/A-18 up to maximum military power. Unlike the heavier Tomcat, the Hornet could launch short of afterburner thrust unless in bomb or strike mode. Today, he was flying in the fighter mode.

The blast deflector shield rose behind the two firetails streaming off the Hornet's GE-404 engines. Forward of Sacrette's cockpit the launch officer knelt on the deck, checking the flaps, ailerons, and launch bar. When certain all was ready, he pointed two fingers down the catapult tracks.

In the so-called bubble, the cat operator watched as the pressure reached the right setting on the massive pistons operating the catapult, and when he was satisfied, he pressed the fire button.

Steam streaked from the track as the Hornet lurched forward. In the cockpit Sacrette was slammed into his seat by the transverse g's working on his body. Within seconds, the strike/fighter was screaming off the deck. The aircraft dipped slightly after clearing the catapult jump ramp, appearing as though the forces of gravity might draw the aircraft into the waiting sea.

In the cockpit Sacrette pushed the throttles through military power into Zone Five afterburner and raised the nose to begin climbing at pure vertical.

Farnsworth stood watching, saying nothing, as he had during a thousand launches. Whatever was the need for the Alert Five would be answered by the CAG.

9

"RED WOLF ONE TO HOME PLATE. CRUISING AT Angels eighteen. Awaiting instructions. Over." Glancing out of the cockpit, he saw three more F/A–18s from the Alert Five flying onto his tail, forming a tactical diamond.

Sacrette rechecked his crypto frequency and listened to the voice of Admiral Lord from the CIC.

"Red Wolf Leader, proceed with Red Wolf pack to coordinates Kilo-seven-four . . . Yankee-five-six."

Sacrette turned on the digital display until the moving map of the coast of Somalia was projecting onto his heads-up display. A unique feature in modern American fighters, the moving display provided an articulated flight chart of the designated area of operation. Once the area was projecting, he punched in the coordinates on the HUD and felt the computer take control of the aircraft.

"Red Wolf One requesting instructions."

"Defend the evacuation force against incoming aircraft," was the order.

Sacrette pressed the mike switch on the HOTAS. "Roger, will fly intercept and provide tactical canopy."

Reaching the coast of Somalia, Sacrette could see the dragonfly shapes of the heavy transport helicopters drifting over the capital city of Mogadishu. In the distance, flying in and out of a pall of smoke that formed a heavy cloud above the city, he saw the distinct shape of two fighter planes.

Sacrette knew it was doubtful that the rebel pilots would fire on the evacuation force. The rebel forces were merely sending a message. This was a message that the rebels were more sophisticated than believed. That they not only had ground forces, but people who could fly fighter aircraft had joined their army, either by choice—or coercion.

But, he thought, he had to be cautious. In the game where second-place finish was no finish at all, he mentally prepared for combat.

"Wolf Pack, go to a two-by-two spread at Angels fifteen. Four-thousand-foot step-up. Red Wolf Two on my three at fifteen. Red Wolf Three and Four, fly TAC. Keep your eyes open and obey the ROE. Rules of engagement are as follows: Do not fire unless fired upon, or certain of eminent attack. Do you copy?"

Flying off his right wing, Rhino reported, "Roger, Thunderbolt. On your three at Angels fifteen." He was constantly turning in his seat, scanning the sky to the rear while Sacrette watched the front. Visibility was made clearer by the unobscured clamshell canopy of the Hornet, which was considered by veteran pilots to be the best canopy in the world of aviation. Only the F–16 Falcon could compete at the same level.

Following standard operating procedures, the two remaining pilots, Stevens and Thomas, rogered the CAG's order.

Moments later the patrol moved from one of caution to dead seriousness. The commander of the lead evacuation helo sounded over the commo frequency. "Red Wolf Leader, be advised, there are two intruders harassing my aircraft."

Sacrette turned on the radar and brought the televised images of the two aircraft onto the screen of his horizontal indicator. Two American-built F–4 Phantom's were flying close to the evacuation squadron. Sighting the Phantoms, which had been replaced in the U.S. Navy by the F–18, was no surprise. Somalia was a pro-western nation; much of the country's military hardware was American. Shooting at the Phantom would not be easy; but certainly not difficult. He loved the old "Double Ugly"; he loved his own life even more.

In the CIC aboard the *Valiant*, the warning of the threat made Admiral Lord reach instinctively for the red telephone linking the carrier with the Joint Chiefs at the Pentagon. Seconds later, the admiral's conversation was being scrambled to the Pentagon, then unscrambled as the Chief of Naval Operations learned of the situation.

"Do not fire unless fired upon. Intent is not to be interpreted. Repeat. Fire only if fired upon."

Lord said nothing. He was angry. To give the enemy the first shot violated one of the most sacred maxims of aerial warfare: *Get off the first shot!* That put the aircraft on the defensive, generally burying the fighter's nose during evasive tactics, denying the pilot the use of his own radar weapons systems to counterattack.

Lord transmitted the CNO's orders.

"Bullshit!" said Sacrette, noting that the line of flight was now over the ocean. "These puppies are over international waters and harassing a U.N.-sanctioned evacuation force. I'm damned if I'll risk my crew and aircraft because of political diplomacy."

"Be advised, Captain—you have your orders." Lord's voice was tinged with the anger and frustration his pilots were experiencing.

"Yes, sir," Sacrette mumbled. Then he switched his weapons system to the mode most preferred by the fighter pilot: guns!

10

AERIAL COMBAT HAS CHANGED LITTLE SINCE THE pioneering tactics were developed by the WWI ace Oswald Boelke:

Secure all possible advantage before attacking.
If you initiate an attack, follow it through.
Fire only at close range.
Keep your eye on your opponent.
Attack your opponent from behind.
If an opponent dives to attack you, turn and meet him.
Remember your line of retreat.
Fly and fight in groups of four or six; if you break into
single combat, don't have several aircraft attacking the same
opponent.

Sacrette decided to test the Somali pilots knowledge at close range. He aimed the nose of his Hornet at the nearest Phantom; Rhino did the same while the other two Americans stayed above the action. Traveling at over six-hundred miles an hour, Sacrette flashed past the first

F-4 close enough to see the pilot in the front seat of the two-seat fighter.

The rear-seat aviator waved as the two aircraft passed. Sacrette laughed, then "bat-turned" sharply, a maneuver the Hornet does better than any aircraft in the sky. In a split second he was on the Phantom's tail.

Playing the buttons on the HOTAS like a piccolo, Sacrette switched to his AIM-9L Sidewinders and began sensing the heat signature with his AN/APG-65 radar. When the targeting box on the HUD turned into a circle, Sacrette knew he had the Somali pilot locked up from heat signature.

He knew something else: the Iraqi would be hearing a chirping in his ear, telling him he was locked up.

The Phantom seemed to fly without intention for a moment; suddenly the Phantom rolled inverted and dove for the sea.

Sacrette stayed with the Phantom, knowing the chirping was driving the pilot and rear-seat officer insane. Waiting to be killed. Decreasing power as the Phantom dove, Sacrette stayed close to the tail, not wanting to fly by and lose the advantage. His years of experience had created a certain intuition in situations such as this, and he figured the Somali was preparing to take him through a double scissors evasive tactic.

Nearing the sea, the Phantom pulled up sharply, decreased airspeed, then did what Sacrette had heard of happening only once; the pilot ejected from the aircraft!

The rear seat blew, then the front. The ejection seat rockets burned brightly as the two Somalis began the wildest ride of their lives.

Not since a Libyan pilot did the same maneuver over the Gulf of Sidra, trying to escape an F-14 Tomcat, had he seen a pilot so out of situational awareness, so totally defeated, with no idea of what to do.

Sacrette could only laugh as the two parachutes deployed; in the distance, the second Phantom was hauling for the coast with both afterburners spewing at full throttle.

11

In the CIC, Lord was watching the air battle on a television monitor where the "real-time" transmission was arriving from Sacrette's television camera mounted in the nose of his Hornet. Laughter from the technicians manning their stations filled the air, forcing Lord to raise his hand for silence. When he spoke into the microphone, his voice was not laced with the enthusiasm of the crew.

"Return to the carrier," the admiral ordered angrily.

Minutes later the four aircraft returned to the *Valiant*. Amid the cheering and hoopla on the flight deck, Sacrette received an order from the air boss. "The admiral wants you and your pilots to report to the bridge."

Turning the aircraft over to the recovery crew, the four pilots reported to the bridge.

"Keep your mouths shut," Sacrette ordered the others. "I'll handle this."

Or so he thought. When the CAG saw the face of the admiral, he knew an ass-chewing would follow.

"That was an insane act on your part, Captain."

Admiral Lord braced the four pilots at attention in the bridge. He turned at just the right moment to suppress a thin smile. Then, when composed, faced again the pilots.

"Have the Somalis reported an incident, sir?" Sacrette asked.

Lord shook his head. "There have been no reports."

"And the pilots?" asked Rhino.

Lord grumped. "They were picked up at sea by a fishing boat."

"That means . . . there was no harm done, sir," Sacrette said. He was trying his damnedest to suppress his laughter.

Admiral Lord didn't reply. Instead, he ordered, "You are excused. I'll expect a written report within the hour."

The pilots saluted and left the bridge.

When alone, Lord looked out across the vast expanse toward Somalia.

Then he laughed his ass off!

12

THE WHITE LIONS ORGANIZATION WAS DIVIDED INTO several factions, each designated with the title *commando*, for the historical Boer fighting units that had served as a rapid deployment force during the Boer War.

The most powerful was the Military Commando, which incorporated the army, air force, and navy. This commando was delegated the duty of infiltrating the entire South African security forces, ascertaining those in the military who could be trusted, who could not, and those who would remain neutral, and there were more of these than the others combined.

The Finance Commando was mainly made up of businessmen and women with a keen eye on the South African economy. Their responsibilities were two fold: raise the necessary funds to form a new South Africa, and have in place an economic structure that was durable enough to ride out the storm of international sanctions that would follow the overthrow of the government and establishment of a new government.

The Political Commando was one of the most important, and it was linked heavily to both the Military and Finance commandos. Its responsibility was to create a broad-based political foundation that would give the new government instant political clout throughout the nation once the overthrow began, until the completion of the insurrection. This included a national government, foreign diplomats, and local government structure. All aspects of government had been considered: health, education, transportation, communications, even the preservation of art. The White Lions, unlike other revolutionary groups in Africa, would not attempt to assume power with nothing more than idealism.

The Science Commando was responsible for the preservation of technology, especially the protection of nuclear power facilities and research facilities; it also handled manufacturing with a specific eye on the vast diamond, gold, and other natural resource mining operations.

The Security Commando was the deadliest. Many of its members were former or present members of Special Branch, agents trained in assassination, interrogation, and terror tactics. The Security Commando would be important in the period following the overthrow, given the task of maintaining covert intelligence gathering within the nation to prevent a counterrevolution. During the period of the overthrow, key white and black leaders had been targeted for assassination and kidnap. These were simply called the troublemakers.

Finally, there was the Cultural Commando, whose responsibility would be the management of the "black problem" which referred to the millions of black South Africans. A plan had been conceived. One requiring the cooperation of all the commandos, especially the Military and Security.

Armed with the vast resources of the nation, the White Lions would be prepared to face whatever the fate of the men and women forging a new South Africa would be. A South Africa born in violence, nurtured in violence, and kept alive through violence.

Sitting in his library at Nagmaal, Coos van Muerwe reflected on the great new trek about to begin. A deeply religious man, he was reading the Bible when the telephone rang.

He listened intently for several minutes before speaking to Shorn, who had completed a late-night session with other legislators in Pretoria.

"It comes as no surprise," he said flatly.

There was a sigh from the other end of the line. Shorn said dejectedly, "We had hoped this matter could be settled peacefully."

"You should have known there was no other way."

"What do you think de Klerk will do?" asked Shorn.

Van Muerwe laughed sharply. "What can he do? Order the military to attack? That's highly unlikely. The military will be on our side—or do nothing at all."

Shorn didn't sound convinced, but he knew the dye had been cast. There was no other way now. "You are instructed to go ahead with Operation Lion's Laager."

Van Muerwe hung up the telephone. Suddenly he felt compelled to visit the one place that had given him strength through the years of planning. But first there was the matter of his men. He had to see them. Speak with them. Be with them in order to make certain of his decision.

He marched out into the warm night where he spent

a few minutes walking around the various military positions. The young White Lions were mostly awake, sensing that something dramatic was approaching. After checking the positions, and offering words of encouragement to the young soldiers, he was convinced the course was one of God's planning.

He climbed into his jeep and drove away from Nagmaal.

In the distance the shadows of the Drakensberg range loomed, calling him to where he knew was the source of his strength. Van Muerwe drove off, not fearing the danger lurking in the night.

He knew he was the only danger the night concealed.

13

2345.

ON A RIDGE NOT FAR FROM NAGMAAL, VAN MUERWE stood where his ancestors had once stood. Had died. What had once been called the Ncome River threaded its way lazily through the mountains of the Drakensberg range, a vaulting mountain range that formed a plateau around the Ncome, although the river was known in South African history by another name: *Blood River*.

February 4, 1838, was the beginning of a legendary hour in the history of South Africa. A vibrant Boer named Piet Retief led 350 Boers and nearly 200 servants on the Great Trek out from Cape Colony into the savage hinterland.

Piet Retief had a vision. A vision of a vast nation ruled by the Afrikaner. A nation of white people in a continent inhabited by black people.

A nation built by whites. For whites.

Reaching Mgungundlovu, the huge royal kraal of the Zulu war chief Dingabe, the brother of Shaka, Retief sought to purchase land for his *voertrekkers*. Retief and seventy-one Boers went into the kraal to negotiate. Dingabe, who feared the Boers were sorcerers, shouted the words that would change the shape of history, both politically and socially, for over two centuries: *"Bulani aba-thakathi!"*

"Kill the wizards!"

Then the slaughter began. Retief and the seventy-one, including his sons and thirty-one black servants, were taken to a nearby hill and brutally murdered. One by one their skulls were crushed ceremoniously by knob-kerrie-wielding warriors. Following the killings, the Zulus swarmed the unsuspecting *voertrekkers*, killing everyone, including 185 children.

Ten months later, a tall, lean Dutchman named Andries Pretorius led a column of 464 riflemen to the banks of the Ncome where he found a narrow plateau guarded on one side by the river, and on the other by a deep ravine.

The Zulus attacked. Twelve thousand screaming, charging tribesmen bent on "washing their assegais" in the blood of the invaders.

When the battle ended over three thousand Zulus lay dead, their nation defeated.

That day was December 16, 1838, a day Pretorius vowed he would "deliver the enemy into our hands . . . we shall observe the day and the date . . . like the Sabbath in His honour."

That day became a national holiday in white South Africa.

That day changed the name of the Ncome River to the name it would be known by from that day afterward: *Blood River!*

Van Muerwe often came to this spot for deliberation. Standing where his ancestors died with the Pretorius column, he was looking down through the rich darkness, and could almost hear the gunfire coming from the laager, the defensive fortification of encircled wagons.

He could almost smell the gunpowder. Taste the blood that turned the river a deep crimson.

He could hear the words shouted by Retief. Words that some say still echo through the night from the hillock at Mgungundlovu: *"Avenge us! Avenge us!"*

He checked his watch. Nearly midnight. He turned to leave, but paused, and looked back to the Blood River.

In a low whisper, he swore to the Afrikaner heritage: "Retief's vision will be preserved."

PART TWO: LION'S LAAGER

14

0400.

On this morning, van Muerwe rose with particular vigor; he had slept little, but feeding on the adren-
aline and expectation, he dressed quickly and went to
his library. Taking several cards from a Rolodex, he carefully dialed three trunk calls. He said nothing to the
voices on the other end, except a cryptic message . . .
"Bring the wagons into laager."

He left the library and walked into the darkness
where he paused beside a military gun jeep. The young
soldier sitting in the turret was Paulus Tuys, a boy he
had watched grow to a man; the son of a man he watched
die in Namibia.

He spoke in Afrikaans. *"Goeie middag my vried. Hoe
gan dit?"*

"Dit gaan goed, dankie. En met jou?"

"I am optimistic," van Muerwe replied. They talked more, in the language he loved. A language banned
in South Africa following the English triumph of the
Anglo-Boer war at the turn of the century. The Boers
had lost, their language was ruled no longer permissible.

The fools! he thought. *You can't destroy a language unless you first destroy the people who created the language.* Afrikaans was a cleansing of the Dutch language; or so the Boers believed. The remnants of the war, the men, women, and children who survived had kept the flame of Afrikaans alive until the rise to power in 1948 of the Afrikan Party. That was the beginning of apartheid, separation of the races, the method advocated by the God they believed had brought them to southern Africa as the new Israelites.

Van Muerwe had no particular feelings about the blacks; they were here to serve the nation, nothing else. The terrorist organization African Nationalist Council had stirred up the blacks and his country was now at the brink of destruction. The world called for an end to the political government. An end that would mean the end of South Africa.

South Africans had historically claimed to be the first inhabitants of the southern tip of the continent; a claim on which they based their right of ownership to the land. Black tribes, claimed the South African historians, had moved into the area after the white Dutch settlers first came ashore. A claim that was largely unsubstantiated by either white or black historians. Such was the basis for the white Afrikaner's self-proclaimed right to rule the area. Blacks were considered by the Afrikaners to be immigrants, as were the people of color brought from India during the nineteenth century to provide a labor work force.

Van Muerwe and the White Lions knew time was the enemy. Time and the weakened state of resolve created by world pressure, internal turmoil, and the constant riotings. The notion of one-man one-vote was a suicidal notion for the White Lions. A notion that would place the white population at the mercy of millions of blacks and people of color who had historically borne the mantle of suppression in South Africa. A bloodbath would ensue, of that he was certain.

Van Muerwe still saw himself as the white Boer of the early years: in South Africa to build a great nation for God.

Much had changed since the beginning of apartheid. World pressure was closing in around the white South Africans. Freedom for the black population was the basis for the U.N. sanctions. Sanctions that had thus far proved ineffective since the wealth of South Africa was too immense in natural resources to be shunned by the world. But what about an uprising? He was convinced that the black population would one day rise and form a powerful military threat to the white government. When that day arrived all would be lost. And who could they turn to?

He knew they had only themselves, and the weapon of surprise.

Soon, like the Boers of the "flying cavalry" commandos of the past, new commandos would ride across the land in great tanks, fly through the air in great war machines, and do what God had intended: build his country.

The name of the new state had been decided: the Free Afrikan Republic.

They would have an economy from the wealthy resources of the Orange Free State, Natal, and the Transvaal. The English descendants could have the Cape Province, and the blacks as well. Blacks would not be permitted to live in the new country. Nor work there. Boers were farmers and they would farm as they had for centuries, with zeal and obedience to the Word of God. The English South Africans could have the blacks and the Afrikaners would make no apology—nor offer any assistance should the Zulu and Xhosa rise again and wash their assegais in blood.

The break would be complete.

Checking his watch, he felt the anticipation. It was time. He walked to the barn where Demlov would be waiting for his final instructions.

He found the Russian dressed in his flight suit. The aircraft was armed with the only weapon needed: the particle beam weapon.

"You know your mission?"

Demlov nodded. "The mission is simple enough. Precisely one of the primary missions the Wolfhound was designed to undertake."

Van Muerwe studied the lines of the transatmospheric aircraft. "You have the times and coordinates for your first target?"

Demlov smiled, and blue-eyed and blond-haired, he looked like any of the other White Lions. But van Muerwe knew he was not. He was a Russian. A communist. Worse, he was a traitor for money. Worse than a mercenary. He despised having to use the Russian, but knew his value was too great. The aircraft would provide the basis for future aircraft of similar design once the nation had been established. The air over Africa would be ruled by van Muerwe's air force.

"When complete . . . return to base. You'll be given another assignment."

Demlov looked up to see the ground crew approaching. He climbed into the cockpit.

Van Muerwe went to his library where he made one

final telephone call. This call was the call he had waited for years to make. "Have you located the Bantu?"

The expression on his face clearly indicated that the question was answered to his satisfaction.

15

0515.

THE WOLFHOUND STREAKED ACROSS THE SKY LIKE A
comet; a low purr followed in its wake as the sleek fighter
struck for the heart of the Cape Province. Port Elizabeth
lay off the left wingtip; the low range of the Great Karroo
Mountains were off the right. Ahead lay the primary
target: Table Mountain, the massive plateau looming
over Cape Town at the tip of the continent.

He was utilizing all his skills as a pilot and all the
technological deceit available to the aircraft. Flying low
to the ground, the Wolfhound was locked into the terrain
avoidance system guiding the fighter over the land; the
system reacted faster than the human mind could com-
prehend.

As the sun etched the eastern horizon, he switched
on a radar tracking system and punched in the digital
frequency of his target. From atop Table Mountain, the
massive communications system, a NASA facility shared
by the South Africans when not used by the Americans
for space purposes, was transmitting and receiving com-

munication via satellites drifting through the heavens beyond the bonds of earth.

With the frequency locked to the Wolfhound, Demlov armed the particle beam weapon.

He pressed the firing mechanism, sending a beam of green-white light flashing to earth.

At the facility, the laser found the sophisticated equipment, instantly melting the optical transmission fibers.

Flying over the site, Demlov could see the facility sat in the darkness before sunrise; a darkness not quite as dark as the current communication capabilities of the South African government.

South Africa was now without microwave communication to the outside world or within South Africa.

———

Tokoza Township. South Africa.

THE INSURRECTION HAD BEGUN. THROUGHOUT
South Africa, tens of thousands of Afrikaners, joined by
an equal number of South Africans of English descent,
began what was called Operation Lion's Laager. In the
black township of Tokoza, none were better prepared
than the black-booted members of the South Africa Police. Young. Lean. Tough. These men had faced years
of terror from the riots of various factions inside and
outside South Africa.

They stood waiting, watching the advance of black
faces marching steadily toward their position, anticipating what all knew would happen.

"Bloody kaffirs!" Sergeant Dirk Ayss's voice hissed
while watching the crowd swelling forward in a wave.
Angry voices punctuated the air above the playground
beyond the barbed-wire fence separating the demonstrators from the squad of SAP commanded by Ayss.

Xhosa tribesmen had been on a rampage for weeks,
burning, looting, murdering rival migrant Zulus now
forted up in the nearby hostel. Riot-trained members of

the SAP had been brought in overnight to quell the disturbance, which was now a full-blown riot.

Which didn't bother Ayss. Rather, it served the purpose to which he was pledged.

A thin smile crept across his sun-tanned face; his eyes twinkled slightly as his hand closed around the pistol grip of his 7.62 caliber FN-FAL automatic rifle.

"Come along, you bastards!" Ayss whispered at the approaching Xhosas.

When the riotors reached a point thirty meters from the fence, Ayss's weapon rose to his shoulder. Simultaneously, his twenty men spread in a nearby formation followed suit as Ayss ordered, "Prepare for attack."

The metallic ring of the automatic weapons' bolts closing rippled through the hot, dusty air as the men waited for the next order.

"Present arms!"

The muzzles were trained on the throng.

Ayss spotted one particular lad; a tall, lanky youth the SAP officer had watched for several days. He wore a T-shirt bearing the face of Nelson Mandela above the crest of the African National Council, a previously outlawed group that had recently pledged to abandon the military overthrow of the South African apartheid government.

The blade of Ayss's front sight centered on the ANC crest.

A hush suddenly fell over the throng. The hesitation was what Ayss suspected.

They need encouragement, the Afrikaner told himself.

That was when Ayss's finger closed around the trigger. The ANC crest suddenly looked torn, then turned red as the young man was thrown backward into the arms of another youth.

A volley of twenty rifles reported with cold, methodical accuracy. Set on semiautomatic, the policemen of the infamous "Black Boots" squad of the SAP took deliberate aim, squeezing off their rounds at specific targets.

The killing zone quickly filled with the screams of the demonstrators; not the wounded, for there were none. All those struck were killed instantly by the precision firing.

Twenty. Forty. Sixty. The death toll stacked up at the front of the throng until the soul was torn from the Xhosas. The retreat began almost immediately.

The report of tear gas being fired was heard; popping canisters of the gas created small clouds along the street, turning the air gray as the gas burned the skin and eyes of the demonstrators.

Babies were trampled, knocked from their mothers' arms. Small children were crushed as the crowd lost control and turned into a fleeing horde.

Ten minutes after the carnage began, the shooting stopped. The "Black Boots" never broke rank, nor pursued. They merely stood calm, killing with impunity until the street was cleared of the living, filled with the dead.

Bodies now lay in small piles, as though purposely placed in such a manner.

That was not the case. Many of the dead had used the bodies of their comrades as a shield but found the accuracy of the "Black Boots" to be more deadly than expected.

When several trucks rolled through the streets to

recover the bodies, Ayss went into the office of the To-koza SAP constable. He took the telephone and made a trunk call.

The voice at the other end was familiar. With obvious glee, Dirk Ayss spoke the chilling words Colonel Coos van Muerwe had waited all morning to hear.

"White Lions!"

17

Springbok Two. Natal.

Dr. Hendrik Brand was thirty-eight, stout, and bearded; a replica of his Boer ancestors who made the trek from the Cape to settle the Transvaal in the 1800s. Educated. Wealthy. Brand was one of the foremost authorities on nuclear fission in South Africa.

He was also the chief scientist and director of the Springbok Project.

South Africa's development of nuclear weapons.

Walking briskly through a security checkpoint in the secretive research building, Brand was followed by Alice Merino, a brilliant young research scientist recently assigned to the project. Alice was thirty, trim, and quite beautiful. The niece of Coos van Muerwe, she had easily secured her position on the project.

At the heavy steel doors blocking the entrance to an elevator, two guards stood at attention. Both relaxed as the scientists approached. Brand noticed the expression on the face of one of the guards. "Is there a problem?"

The guard nodded grimly. "The security roster was

changed. The two guards at the lower level are not the regularly assigned guards."

Brand cursed softly, then looked at Alice.

"We have no choice," was all the scientist said as he nodded to the guard.

Stepping to a digital panel, one guard punched a series of numbers into the control panel marked VAULT. Seconds later the pneumatic horizontal locks released and the doors swung open. Entering the elevator, Brand and Merino pressed the single button on the panel.

The sound of the steel doors closing was heard for only a few moments as the elevator began its two-hundred-foot descent into the bowels of Springbok Two.

Brand checked his watch. "We have precisely eighteen minutes. Are you certain you know what to do?"

Alice nodded sharply. "I know my responsibilities." Casually, her hand slipped into the deep pocket of her white smock.

Before Brand could say another word they felt the elevator slow to a stop. The doors opened to another set of heavy doors. They waited, then saw the doors open. Two more guards stood waiting. Both carried automatic weapons. Both were strangers.

"Good afternoon, Dr. Brand," said one of the guards, an older man wearing the uniform of the South African army.

A younger guard checked the security badge on Alice Merino, noting how her large breasts tilted her badge to one side on her white smock.

Bloody nice pair of tits, he thought to himself. She smiled softly, as though knowing his thoughts. Knowing something else more important than the size of her breasts: That would be the last thought he would ever have.

As though programmed the right hands of the two scientists rose simultaneously. Both held automatic pistols. Silencers were threaded to the muzzles, suppressing the weapons' reports as both pistols fired.

The guards stumbled backward, their knees going slack, then crumpled to the concrete floor. The scientists stood for a long moment, staring pitifully at the dead men. Neither was a killer, and until this moment had not been certain they had the resolve to carry through the mission.

"Come. We must hurry," ordered Brand.

Passing through another set of security doors, Brand found eight scientists waiting. All were handpicked over the past year to join the Springbok Project.

All were Afrikaner.

An hour later eight large crates were transported to the surface by elevator. The two guards at the surface, both distant cousins of Brand's, stood watch while the crates were loaded aboard a lorry. Within minutes the lorry passed through a series of checkpoints manned by South African soldiers loyal to Coos van Muerwe and the White Lions.

Two hundred feet below the surface, one of Brand's technicians completed the final phase of the mission.

In the nuclear storage vault of Springbok Two, Brand pressed a button on an arming device.

He looked at Alice Merino, telling her, "The remaining weapons are now armed with a tamper proof detonation device."

Alice went to a telephone and dialed a trunk number. When the voice answered at the other end, she said, *"White Lions."*

18

IN VAN MUERWE'S LIBRARY A BANK OF TELEPHONES had been installed and were being manned by a dozen young men and women wearing khaki shirts and shorts, the uniform of the White Lions.

On the right sleeve was a patch bearing the emblem of a white lion; three arrows, bent to a ninety-degree angle, framed the face of the lion, giving the creature the look of being set within spokes.

Or, as some opponents pointed out heatedly, a swastika.

Moira Prouse, Van Muerwe's daughter, was blond, blue-eyed, and athletically trim. She was a former member of the South African Olympic swim team, and her movements were lithe, almost feline. She was beautiful. Powerful.

Widowed at twenty-three, she continued to treasure the memory of her husband, Captain Vernon Prouse, a pilot in van Muerwe's squadron during the war in Namibia. Three days before the withdrawal of the South

African army from Namibia, Prouse was killed by a SAM missile.

She survived the loss by becoming fiercely involved in what she, her father, and thousands of Afrikaners believed was their only hope for the future: the White Lions.

Unlike her brother Pieter, a disappointment to the colonel, Moira was the focus of her father's pride. His "lioness," as he was often heard proclaiming.

She was, many commented, the mirror image of her father.

Looking up from the telephone nestled into the crook of her shoulder, she motioned to a young lieutenant standing at a large map depicting South Africa.

Malcolm Erasmus, a neighbor and childhood friend, approached with a grin. "The reports are spectacular!"

Moira covered the mouthpiece of the telephone. "I know. I have another report. From Soweto. Riots have broken out in the streets. The police are unable to control the situation. The army is being called in to take action." There was a sheepish grin. "I wonder who had that assignment?"

Erasmus shook his head. Laughing, he replied, "I don't know. But they did the job."

He left and went back to his map and drew a red circle around Soweto. A cheer erupted from the others. Dozens of cities, townships, and military installations were circled in red.

The operation code-named Lion's Laager had begun.

The entire nation was now under insurrection. Insurrection created by the White Lions.

Down the hall from the library, in his private office,

Coos van Muerwe heard the cheers. He turned to a group of men wearing a variety of uniforms of the South African defense forces.

"Gentlemen, you are to be congratulated. Operation Lion's Laager has begun. At this moment the entire nation is in chaos. Riots. Roads blocked. Cities without power. Transportation at a standstill. The first step toward our homeland is complete."

He raised a glass of wine and toasted the officers. Then, he turned to the only other man in the room not wearing a uniform.

"The next phase of the operation will begin tonight." He raised his glass and toasted the heavyset man standing in the corner.

Jan Roos, the commander of the Security Commando, bowed graciously to his host.

19

Tuynhuys. Cape Town. South Africa. 2200.

IN THE EXECUTIVE MANSION OVERLOOKING THE southern port city, the President of South Africa had been on the telephone the entire afternoon, and now through the evening. Reports were coming in from military bases, police stations, and provincial capitals. What had been considered the worse possible scenario was developing: Right-wing Afrikaner extremists were laying claim to what they considered their birthright.

The Transvaal. The Free Orange State. Natal.

"The situation is becoming uncontrollable, Mr. President. My Cabinet is threatening to resign. The majority of the military is now under the control of right-wing extremists. Those not under control are refusing to raise arms against their brother South Africans. Throughout the country paramilitary groups have taken up military positions in key areas. Railroad lines have been cut. Factories have closed. Communications have been destroyed with few exceptions. The population—white and black—have never been further apart than this moment.

God! The ANC is threatening to launch a counterrevolution."

President F. W. de Klerk paused while the President of the United States responded with the obvious, but least likely solution to his problem.

After considering the suggestion, de Klerk replied, "The Secretary General of the United Nations has been notified. In light of the sanctions and political status of the South African government it's obvious we will not be assisted by the United Nations. No, Mr. President, we can expect no assistance from the outside world."

"What form of assistance are you requesting from the United States, Mr. President?" There was a near hopeless tone in the American President's voice.

The most difficult words ever spoken by de Klerk rolled from his lips. "We need military assistance until the insurrection is suppressed. Our forces still loyal to the government are vastly outnumbered."

The American President straightened in his chair and laid his cards squarely on the table. "The people of the United States will boil me in oil if I send troops to assist South Africa. You know the feelings of America toward apartheid. Toward your government."

Remembering their frank discussions on de Klerk's recent trip to the United States, the South African President played his hole card. "The alternative is much worse, Mr. President. If the government is taken over by the radicals there will be a bloodbath in this country the likes of which have not been seen since Hitler. Apartheid will be replaced by genocide! Tell that to your people."

"Christ," the President of the United States muttered.

Feeling he had an opening, de Klerk pushed his position. "You should know the black African units have refused unequivocally to assist the security forces."

The President said aloud what both men knew. "Which could mean the black forces might join with the ANC. That would involve American troops in a racial war. You know the American people would never stand for such a possibility. My God, Congress would eat me blood raw."

De Klerk knew the President was correct. He also knew there was one possibility that the American Congress might find acceptable.

"There may be a way. One your people would find acceptable. What if I could assure your Congress that the ANC and the black population will not become involved?"

"How can you do that?"

"There is an organization. A secretive organization I've been made aware of. The Black Peace Coalition. The Coalition is attempting to organize a black leadership infrastructure composed of all the black leaders. Along with this leadership will be the formulation of a plan that will provide certain guarantees to both white and black."

"Who is the head of the Coalition?"

"There's no head per se, but a man named Michael Loweta is the liaison. He and a white South African named Andrew Gable."

De Klerk's intelligence apparatus had reported weeks before that Michael Loweta, a young black attorney, had been selected by the black leaders to mold the black factions into a single political entity. Which meant he had a means of contacting the black leaders at this time, most of whom were probably in hiding.

There was a long pause. Finally, the U.S. President added to the menu. "It'll take more than that. You'll need the leadership from the Homelands to guarantee that they will not get involved."

"In other words, a purely white versus white confrontation." De Klerk's voice was flat but emphatic.

"That's correct. White versus white. Your white troops versus the white Afrikaners. I don't like the thought. I dislike the thought of white versus black much more. But it's the way it must be."

"I'm afraid I don't have any white troops, Mr. President. A general stand down is occurring in the military. What few troops I can count on are being rounded up by the White Lions."

De Klerk glanced out the window. In the distance the glow of a few sporadic fires etched the dark African night. Rioting had been kept to a minimum since the White Lions did not want to ruin their credibility by destroying the cities. Instead, they were assisting in the suppression of rioters. Nonetheless, there was the wail of sirens, the stammer of machine-gun fire, and the roar of aircraft filtered through into his office.

The White Lions were taking control. Systematically. Methodically. In the most cunning fashion: taking great care not to do injury to their political base. And he knew who was at the core of the insurrection. A man he had known most of his life. Coos van Muerwe. A national hero. A man who once he set out on a mission was not dissuaded so long as there was life in his body.

The White Lions would prevail, of this he was certain. A certainty that seemed to cement his resolve. He told the President of the United States, "I'll send my representative straightaway to find Mr. Loweta. But it may take some time."

"You must find him and convince him to intercede. Otherwise, I won't be able to convince my people that the black population won't wind up in the middle of this situation."

As he hung up the telephone, de Klerk sat back heavily into his chair. He was about to make another telephone call when he looked up to see a man enter his office.

"Excuse me, sir." Ted Lyons, de Klerk's chief of security, stood in the doorway looking nervous. Ted Lyons was a bronze-skinned former game preserve superintendent. Their friendship stretched back through the years, to the time before de Klerk became a national political figure. He was the one man the President felt he could trust at this moment.

"Yes, Ted?"

"Your car is outside, Mr. President. A helicopter is waiting at the airport. You have to leave. Immediately. Intelligence reports indicate a large paramilitary group is en route to this office. Your life may be in danger."

De Klerk pulled himself heavily from his leather chair and smoothed his face, trying to rub away the fatigue. The truth. He gave momentary thought to the possibility of staying, of trying to establish a dialogue with van Muerwe through his loyal soldiers. Perhaps the bloodshed could be avoided. Then he heard the sirens, and knew that once the floodgates had been opened, the wave of emotion that would be sweeping the white population could not be contained by reason.

It would require the use of force to meet force. A force that he could not be certain was at his disposal.

"My God," he whispered. "Is this really happening, Ted?"

"I'm afraid so, Mr. President." He was carrying a briefcase. The briefcase contained a telephone that the President could use in trying to quell the disturbance. One of the numbers coded into the telephone was the number of the American embassy. The American embassy was waiting at this moment to receive the President of South Africa.

De Klerk nodded grimly, then followed his security chief to the automobile. They drove to the helipad and minutes later an Alouette lifted off the ground from the rear of the President's mansion for the ride to the Airport where a jet would be waiting to fly him to Pretoria.

Looking down, de Klerk saw patches of fires spreading from the base of Table Mountain toward the seaport. Flashing red and blue lights spotted the streets.

His country was on fire.

Which jerked him to the reality, and the need for action. He took the briefcase and removed a telephone. Seconds later he was speaking to one of his men in Johannesburg.

"Find Mr. Loweta. Tell him it's urgent I speak with him."

20

2348.

ANDREW GABLE DROVE WILDLY THROUGH THE CHA-
otic streets of the black township servicing the Transvaal
white community of Pietermaritzburg. Gable, a businessman in Pietermaritzburg, glanced at his daughter
Patricia, a student, who was staring wildly at the flaming
ruins of the township.

"Oh, God. I can't believe this is happening."

Gable said nothing; he turned and quickly looked
into the backseat, then to the rearview mirror. His
thoughts began to run wild as he saw the lights of a car
following closely behind.

He took a deep breath, then sighed heavily and
reached for his daughter's hand. Beneath her blond hair,
her blue eyes reflected the sadness he had seen only once
in his daughter; the sadness found the day her mother
died. "You have been a brave girl all these years, my
dear. You've risked your freedom and your life more than
most. But you must remember that tonight is different;
tonight, we must not fail. Tonight is too important. It's

what we have prepared for, hoping this moment would never come."

She couldn't help but notice there was a certain strangeness in his voice. Not fear, since that had long been rooted from his system during his years of imprisonment at St. Alban's prison, and then the banning order of 1983 under Section 29 of the Internal Security Act.

He spoke in a calm, orderly voice, as though he had prepared for this moment for years. Like a man watching a sick child he knew one day would die before adulthood.

Then she looked out the window of the car and knew that day had come.

The rioting had started that afternoon and Gable, still restricted to his home, had gone to the meeting that night although he knew it was illegal. A meeting that was very important.

That was where he received word the White Lions had begun the systematic takeover of the government. The country.

"What is the situation, Father? Is the government in control?"

Gable kept his eyes on the taillights in the rearview mirror while he explained what he knew.

"The extremist forces have taken the countryside, leaving the major cities alone. In a sense, the cities are cut off. With the countryside in their control, the White Lions are apparently going to play a waiting game."

"Waiting game? What are they waiting for?"

"For a general uprising of the white population."

"Will that happen?"

He shrugged. "It's already happening. Colonel van Muerwe issued a statement this afternoon offering the white South Africans the opportunity to join his forces.

Tens of thousands have responded by joining."

"What about the army?"

"Mutiny, for the most part. The army and air force have stood down. Almost to a man. They refuse to fight against brother South Africans."

"Van Muerwe knew the military wouldn't support the government." Her words were more statement than thought.

Before he could respond an ear-shattering crack ripped through the air. A spiderweb appeared on the windshield where a bullet passed from the rear window across the front seat.

Patricia screamed.

Gable reached into his briefcase lying on the seat of the car. Hurriedly, he removed a notebook and gave it to Patricia. Looking ahead, he saw a street that was dark.

"At the corner, I'll turn left. You open the door and jump. Go to Ruth Mathatheta's house. She'll hide you."

Patricia turned as another bullet struck the car. Reaching into the backseat, she touched a blanket lying on the floor. There was movement, then from beneath the blanket a familiar voice ordering, "Do as your father says, child."

Patricia took the notebook and, grasping the door handle, waited for the car to swerve at the corner.

Another shot raced harmlessly through the car.

At the corner, Gable swerved left, slowed momentarily to allow his daughter to jump. The door flew open, and she was gone in the swirl of dust as he instantly mashed down on the accelerator.

"Did she make it?" asked the voice from the backseat.

Gable wasn't sure but he saw the lights of the pursuit car were closing and had not stopped.

"I think so."

"What now?" asked the voice.

Gable laughed. "We drive the bloody wheels off this car."

There was a pause. "Thank you, my friend."

Before Gable could reply he saw the lights of the car come alongside. There was a gunshot. The steering wheel flew wildly in his hands. Out of control, the car careened right, then left, crashing against the pursuit car.

Gable's eyes widened.

A building!

The car struck the building at over forty miles an hour. Gable slammed into the steering wheel; he heard the crack of his ribs, felt the rush of air from his lungs. He tried to breathe.

Nothing.

The lights of the pursuit car were now to the rear. A blizzard of white, tormenting artificial light. Through the haze Gable looked in the rearview mirror. The eerie shadows of men could be seen faintly. But clearly, in their hands, as they stepped to the door of the car, he could see pistols.

Looking up through the window, Gable saw the hand of one man rise. The hand gripped a heavy pistol. Behind the pistol, the man leered a smile Gable knew all too well.

A smile that had filled the front page of every newspaper in South Africa on more than one occasion.

Jan Roos. The heavyset assassin of Special Branch, Roos had been thrown out of the service after a nationwide scandal involving the murder of innocent prisoners during interrogation. He had become an embarrassment to the government, a recruitable asset to the White Lions.

Gable tried to rise, but there was no strength. In his last moments he defended himself with his only weapon: the deep-cover agent for Amnesty International smiled.

He smiled in victory.

Standing surrounded by the flames, Roos fired his pistol, silencing one of the enemies of the White Lions.

21

0110.

ADMIRAL ELROD LORD STRAIGHTENED IN THE BUNK of his sea cabin. The admiral's sea cabin was near the bridge, allowing the ship's commander to reach the bridge within seconds should he be needed in an emergency. The term emergency was an understatement.

On the red phone, Lord listened attentively while wiping the sleep from his eyes. A man accustomed to being awoken in the early hours by emergencies he was waking fast as he listened to his orders. What he heard was almost incomprehensible.

"Yes, sir," he replied, then picked up the receiver of the intraship telephone system. One by one, beginning with the CAG, Lord summoned each squadron commander and the captains of the battle group support ships to the main operations center.

Throughout the carrier, the fighting men of the *Valiant* were being awakened. Nothing was said except that the carrier was now at a state of high alert.

An hour later the captains and squadron commanders were assembled. Each shared the look of confusion.

Only one of them knew the nature of the meeting.

Captain Boulton Sacrette had acted immediately. The first aircraft to launch was the E-2 Hawkeye, the carrier-based AWAC that would provide the eyes and ears of the battle group. The Hawkeye, also called Hummer, was approaching its station off the southern coast of South Africa. Along with the Hummer were four F-14 Tomcats and two KA6 Intruders for refueling.

Within minutes of the orders from the CNO, the *Valiant* was already taking a fighting posture as the captains hurried to their heloes for the ride to the briefing.

"What's the situation?" Jugs asked Sacrette.

The CAG said nothing. He just nodded toward a seat, which she quietly took.

After the arrival of the captains, the leaders of the battle group were sitting at the long table commanded by Lord, listening in disbelief to the report which was now being updated every ten minutes from the U.S. Embassy in Pretoria.

" 'The South Africa Police report that the nation is now in complete rebellion. Riots in the white cities and black townships.

" 'The Jan Smuts Airport in Johannesburg has been taken by white radicals loyal to an Afrikaner extremist group.

" 'Cape Town is now under marshal law established by the extremists. The President of South Africa has taken refuge in the American embassy.

" 'Paramilitary units have roadblocked all highways leading to and from black townships and the tribal homelands of Transkei, Lesotho, Bophuthatswana, Ciskei, and Venda. Thousands are reported dead. Many more thousands reported wounded.

" 'Diplomats assigned to foreign embassies and consulates have been ordered to their respective embassies, where they are under 'protective' custody of paramilitary units.

" 'The presidents of Zimbabwe, Mozambique, and Zambia have offered military assistance to the African National Council.' "

Lord put down the communiqué. He stared into the equally dismayed faces of his commanders, then said, "Gentlemen, we are about to enter the most difficult military situation this nation has faced since the Civil War."

There was a long silence. The ramifications couldn't have been more obvious if they had been painted on the walls.

"What exactly are our orders?" asked Captain Asa Clemens of the Aegis-class nuclear-guided missile cruiser *Larimore*.

"We are to get under way immediately to our new station fifty miles off the coast of South Africa in the Indian Ocean."

"And what are we to do once we reach our station?" asked Captain Frank Peterson, a black captain of a marine amphibious assault ship. There was a sincere look of concern on his tough features.

"The CNO has ordered our battle group to lend direct military assistance to the sovereign government of South Africa."

A grumble rolled along the table. "In what manner?" asked a Marine Corps colonel.

Lord straightened abruptly. "In whatever manner is requested by the President of South Africa and approved by the President of the United States."

More grumbling. Finally, Sacrette spoke. He was blunt and to the point. "You expect our battle group to assist a racist government in recovering control of their government?"

Lord stared icily at Sacrette. He felt like a man fighting with snowballs against an enemy with a machine gun. "I expect you to carry out the orders of the CNO and the President of the United States."

"You run the risk," Captain Peterson said softly, but assertively, "of having the first battle group in U.S. naval history to find itself in wholesale mutiny. And I know I don't speak for just the two thousand or more black sailors and marines under your command. I speak for the entire battle group. White and black."

Heads bobbed noticeably along the table. Sacrette merely returned Lord's icy stare. He had lost too damned many good men—black and white—fighting against the evil of domineering governments to see his air wing torn apart by what he knew could occur: refusal to fight!

Lord sat heavily into his chair. Finally, when he spoke, it was not with strength. Nor apology. But with hope. "It is my belief, and the Commander in Chief's belief, that if this rebellion is not stopped, a far greater disgrace than apartheid will happen. Hundreds of thousands—perhaps millions—of men, women, and children will die, be maimed, or suffer, and the hope of democracy will be lost forever. Granted, the government of South Africa is certainly racist, but the hope has been that their policy would change. And it has changed. Slowly. But change has occurred. It's the hope of continual change that has sparked this current situation. Forces are in the field who have stood opposed to democracy, and now—

quite possibly—those forces could prevail." He stopped, then slammed his palm on the table and corrected himself. "No! Not *could* prevail . . . will prevail! If by no other means than by fear and separation."

22

0300.

COLONEL COOS VAN MUERWE COULDN'T SLEEP. HE
had paced constantly around the bunker beneath the
hangar at Nagmaal, anticipating what he knew was coming. The command center had been moved to the bunker
in anticipation of aerial bombardment. Bombardment
that thus far was nonexistent.

I was right! he thought to himself. *The air force will
not bomb. They may not join our forces—not yet—but they
won't obey the Pretoria government! Not against the force that
offers the white South Africans their only salvation!*

An excited young officer approached. "The helicopter is arriving, Colonel."

Van Muerwe clapped his hands together resound-
ingly, then went to the desk he used in the center of the
command post. He took a cigar; a Cuban cigar given him
by a German businessman several weeks earlier during
a visit to Frankfort. He rolled the cigar between his
fingers, then clipped off the tip. Striking a match, he
held the flame, beneath the end and puffed heartily.

A few minutes later, through a cloud of smoke, he

saw three men approaching. One man walked in the middle; two more men walked at his elbows.

As the figure approached the desk, van Muerwe knew that the greatest moment in Afrikaner history was at hand.

"Release him," ordered van Muerwe.

Roos, smiling like a demon, released the handcuffs holding his prisoner. Arrogantly, he pushed the prisoner forward.

The prisoner stepped into the brilliance of a light hanging above van Muerwe's desk.

Van Muerwe studied the face of the prisoner. The light glistened off the prisoner's head, giving a stately iridescence to the man's features. What he noticed most was the absence of fear.

Reaching to the desktop, van Muerwe grabbed a *sjambok*, a long whip.

"What is your name, kaffir?" asked van Muerwe.

The prisoner gave his name.

Van Muerwe's eyes widened. His arm flashed up, then down, bringing the *sjambok* across the prisoner's face.

The prisoner stumbled back, but was immediately thrust forward against the desk when Roos kneed him in the spine.

"No, my dear kaffir. You answered incorrectly. I want to hear your name spoken in the old way. The old way. That means you first say: 'bantu.' Then your name. Do you understand?"

The prisoner showed no reaction. Again the *sjambok* struck him, this time across the chest.

"Say it . . . 'bantu.' Then your name."

The interrogation went on for nearly a half hour.

The prisoner still refusing to denegrate his dignity by the police-state reference of "bantu." A classification no longer required of black Africans when giving their names.

That was part of the old method. The old system. Before de Klerk and the whites who knew changes must come.

Changes van Muerwe refused to accept.

Finally, van Muerwe stepped from around the desk and pulled the bleeding, beaten man to his feet.

"Such arrogance, kaffir."

The prisoner smiled.

This enraged van Muerwe, but instead of hitting the man again, he leaned forward and whispered the classification *for* the prisoner.

"Your name—your correct name—is Bantu . . . Michael Loweta."

In the light before the desk, in the storm of hatred in which he was imprisoned, Michael Loweta shook his head.

With a smile he said, "My name is *Mr.* Michael Loweta."

PART THREE: AMABUTHU

23

RUTH MATHATHETA'S SMALL HOUSE WAS FRAMED IN the darkness of the township, where the early morning continued to ring with the fury of the screaming voices of the enraged citizens. Troops with uniforms of the White Lions had surrounded the township and were now warning the citizens against reprisal if they were caught outside.

"This is insanity," Ruth said softly to the young woman sitting beside her near the window. Patricia Gable leaned forward from the weathered chair in the small front room of Ruth's home and stared past the woman to the red glare of fires flickering against the sky.

"I'm very sorry about your father. He was a good man. A decent man."

Patricia said nothing. She was still in shock from the incident. Moreover, she had no idea why she was here, or what she would do next.

The loud blare of a voice in English warned the population again to remain in their homes. The metallic voice sent a chill threading along Patricia's spine.

Ruth looked curiously at Patricia. "What are you going to do?"

Patricia shook her head. She had seen her father murdered, and her nation was now caught in the grips of an overthrow. She couldn't imagine what she would say in response to the question.

"Your father would not want you to stay here. He would want you to get out of here and find a place where you would be safe."

She shook her head defiantly. "No. I saw him murdered by those bloody bastards. He wouldn't want me to be safe. He would want me to *do* something."

Ruth placed her hands around Patricia's face, and said lovingly, "Child, what can you do?"

Patricia looked at the notebook. "I have Mr. Loweta's notebook. If I can contact his people, they'll know how to contact the other members of the coalition."

"What coalition?" asked Ruth.

"The Black Peace Coalition. My father and other members of the tribes have been trying to establish a coalition of united black representatives. Their goal was to approach the South African government with a realistic plan that would lead our country toward democracy. A plan that would not threaten the white South Africans."

"I've never heard of such a coalition."

"You couldn't have. It's a secret organization. It's not ready to begin negotiations. Their first goal was to stop the factional warfare between the black population. Afterward, they would approach the government for serious discussions."

"And what does Mr. Loweta have to do with the coalition?"

"Mr. Loweta has acted as the liaison between the

various factions. He's the only one they trusted."

Ruth said nothing. Michael Loweta was one of the trusted aids to Nelson Mandela; Loweta was considered one of the more effective voices ameliorating the tribal disputes between the various warring tribal factions. A Zulu, Loweta was probably the only man who knew the whereabouts of Nelson Mandela and other black leaders at this moment.

"You saw Michael Loweta taken by the White Lions. He's either being held someplace very protected, or he could already be dead." There wasn't the slightest sound of hope in her voice.

The thought had crossed her mind. But somehow she thought he was still alive.

"I have to try," Patricia said in a pleading tone.

Ruth thought for a long moment. Finally, she rose from the chair and went to her room where she returned with two long shawls.

"Here," she said, handing one of the shawls to Patricia. "Put this over your head and around your shoulders."

Patricia did as she was instructed.

"Walk close behind me and say nothing. If someone stops us, run back to this house and hide in the bedroom."

Patricia nodded, then followed her housekeeper into the raging night.

"Where are we going?" Patricia asked.

"To find someone."

"Who?"

Ruth paused, then whispered as though revealing some great secret, "The *Amabuthu*."

24

0800.

ABOARD THE *VALIANT*, THE CREW WAS STUNNED AT THE revelation the battle group was deploying to the coast of South Africa. The full gamut of emotions was run, from doubt to fear, concern to frustration.

None were more concerned than a ranking noncommissioned officer whose job it was to coordinate the orders from the top of the chain of command to the men who would carry out those orders at the bottom of the chain.

What was necessary through the chain of command was clarification.

The clarification began with the code-naming of the effort: Operation Blood River.

Ironically, the author of the operational code designation knew nothing of the Ncome River—or the battle and the slaughter of Retief's wagon train. He had, however, heard the reference to Blood River years before while having lunch with the South African attaché while both men were stationed in London. More importantly, he knew that a river of blood would run in South Africa;

therefore, the name was fitting.

By the time the trickle-down effect of the vague order had become graphically clear, the USS *Valiant* was steaming at flank speed with sixteen other ships, thousands of U.S. marines and warplanes, toward the coast of southeast Africa.

This created a dilemma aboard the carrier and throughout the battle group: a lot of the sailors were black African-Americans who were keenly aware of the political situation in the apartheid state. The rift started as a tremor, threading through the battle group until the tremor was about to blow the lid off the Richter scale. It was necessary to obtain more clarification. To the enlisted men the source of clarification was through the chief petty officers.

"I don't give a fuck what anybody says, Diamonds, I'm not fighting for white supremacists. I grew up in Alabama. I've seen the Klan. Orders or no orders—I'm not fighting for a white supremacist government that's making slaves out of African brothers. I'll fight the Russians. Cubans. Colombians. Iraqis. But not for the South Africans."

A grumble of support rippled through the air. Support that made Diamonds think of the scourge of the navy: mutiny.

The black man who spoke was Seaman First Class Albert Mather, one of Diamonds's plane captains. The plane captains were responsible for care and maintenance of the aircraft.

Aircraft that would soon be flying into South Africa in support of the apartheid government.

Diamonds shook his head. "I understand your feelings. I can empathize with what you're saying. But you have to look at this situation objectively. You won't be fighting for the South African government. You'll be fighting for the government of the United States. You'll be fighting against Afrikaner extremists who are taking over the government. If they become the new government, the black Africans will suffer worse."

Diamonds was sitting with a group of men in the "bird coop," a hundred-plus bunk bay for enlisted men of the VFA-101 squadron. The makeup was multiracial: black, Hispanic, and white.

At 0600 the battle group had been ordered from its Persian Gulf duty to the coast of South Africa with instructions to await further orders. The news of what was happening in South Africa was being transmitted by television satellite to the *Valiant*. There was no doubt the carrier was being sent to support the de Klerk government.

The white apartheid government of South Africa.

"That changes nothing. We'll still be supporting the white-controlled government. I don't trust them, Diamonds. I've got a bad feeling this is going to wind up being a racial war." Mather looked around at his nonblack shipmates. "Getting involved in this shit could tear *our* country apart."

Diamonds shook his head. "No more than Korea or Nam was a race war against Asians. Or Panama was racial against Hispanics. Hell, in Grenada, the army was mostly black. Black and Hispanic."

Mather shook his head. "Yeah, but we ain't never fought *for* a government that suppresses the freedom of black people."

Another sailor spoke up, asking, "What if the ANC attacks? That could change the mood of the whole white population supporting de Klerk. Our people could wind up caught between the two factions."

Diamonds thought about that for a moment. "The African National Council has not indicated that it will get involved. I think they're smart enough to ride this thing out and let the devil take the hindmost. The operation is directed toward restoring political and social control to the current government. Without that control, there will be a race war. And it will be bloody."

"Yes," said Mather. "But what if . . . ?

Diamonds had thought of that as well: *What if?*

25

1200.

AT THE MASSIVE PORT IN DURBAN, THE MAN WALKING down the gangway had a noticeable limp. He carried a seabag on his shoulder and seemed to be peering at the debarkation ramp as he descended from the freighter carrying West German registry. In fact, Major Viktor Tragor wasn't watching where he stepped; nor was the limp genuine. He was scanning the deck below, careful to notice if he was being observed.

He appeared free from scrutiny, except for a stevedore on the dock. The burly worker wore a green-striped T-shirt with the springbok on the front. Recognizing the SA national symbol, Tragor knew he had found his contact.

After passing through customs, Tragor went to the front of the Port of Entry and found the stevedore leaning on the hood of a car. They said nothing. Both men entered the car and drove away.

An hour later Tragor was on the north side of Durban, in the home of a woman he had known for nearly twenty years.

Rhoda Zweel was forty-five; she wore her dark hair long and loose over her shoulders, framing a deep bronze face. Her green eyes twinkled at seeing Tragor.

They spoke in Afrikaans, but whispered their greetings in Russian. He sensed a longing in her for the language. One she had rarely spoken since arriving in South Africa as a member of the KGB's Illegals Division. A division once headed by Tragor, Rhoda Zweel was now the Resident.

"The city is in chaos. Troops are constantly on the move. I'm surprised you were allowed in the country," she said while pouring him tea.

"I wasn't certain we would be allowed to make port. But the harbormaster granted permission." He paused, then grew serious. "The state of emergency has created an unexpected obstacle."

Rhoda smiled the kind of smile that didn't seem to particularly reflect concern.

That caught Tragor's attention. "Is there something I should know?"

"The emergency may be the opportunity you need to complete your mission."

"How?"

"South Africa is a country that has always been run very efficiently. That efficiency has been all but destroyed. Movement is not as difficult as you might think. Once you're outside the city, you can move quite freely. The government is trying to control the cities. The extremists control the countryside, the highways, railways, and major air routes."

Tragor understood. "All I need is to get out of the city. You can make the arrangements?"

She nodded. "What then?"

"I'll find the Wolfhound. First Directorate suspected the aircraft was stolen by the South African government. That's now doubtful."

"The extremists?"

"Who else?"

"My thoughts exactly."

"Where will you begin the search?"

Tragor pulled his fingers slowly through his hair. His thoughts drifted back to a dossier he began building years ago. The dossier belonged to a prominent Afrikaner soldier. A soldier whose name was now on the lips of every South African. "I suspect the logical answer lies with Colonel Coos van Muerwe. He's a pilot. And from what I learned about the NASA facility, that was a particle beam attack. He's already begun deploying the Wolfhound. If I find van Muerwe . . . the Wolfhound won't be far away."

"In that case, you'll need more than a way out of the city."

She went to a closet and separated some hanging clothes. A secret room was concealed behind the closet wall. She led him into a small room where she handed him a uniform.

"One of our operatives has infiltrated the White Lions. He gave me one of his uniforms. He will be your contact."

The uniform was sand-colored. On the shoulder was a patch bearing the insignia of the White Lions.

"Do you know where van Muerwe lives?"

Tragor felt certain he knew where he would find the colonel. "Coos van Muerwe was one of my primary focuses during my stay as Resident. I watched him with keen interest before the Special Branch got on my trail.

At one point, I nearly had him assassinated. It comes as no surprise to me that van Muerwe's behind the insurrection. I predicted as much a year ago. But the people in Moscow wouldn't listen."

"Where do you think he'll be during the insurrection?"

"I suspect he'll no doubt be at his farm. It's a bloody fortress. He's in a fight to the death. He'll choose to win or lose on his family ground. Hopefully, the contact will have more details. If I find van Muerwe—I find the Wolfhound. And Demlov."

"What are your orders regarding Demlov?"

Tragor said nothing. Rather, he asked coldly, "Who is the contact?"

Rhoda handed him a piece of paper. A name, an address in Pietermaritzburg, and a telephone number.

"I haven't spoken with the contact since the insurrection began. I assume he's in Pietermaritzburg. That's where he lives."

Tragor thought about what she had said. His voice carried surprise as he noted, "Then you were caught off guard by the insurrection?"

She nodded severely. "There was no warning. Nothing indicated that the Afrikaners would dare pull such a stunt. Not even the government had prior warning. It just suddenly blew up around everyone's head."

He noticed she seemed reluctant to continue. "What are you thinking?"

She looked at her fingers for a moment; admiringly, then clapped hard, as though trying to shock away the truth she now believed. "I think they are going to succeed. If they do, our operation in the country will have to be abandoned."

He understood. "You don't want to return to Russia?"

She laughed acidly. "Did you?"

He had not. After living in the beauty, openness, and richness of South Africa, returning to the dismal, economically and politically bankrupt Soviet Union was worse than any hell he imagined.

Beauty for the Beast.

He said nothing to her for a long, silent moment. Finally, when he spoke, it was the only words that could have really shaken her to the core of her being. She listened until he finished, not interrupting or pointing out the obvious dangers.

At first, she thought him insane. After further consideration, she knew it was an option she had not had before his arrival. One she would never have considered, or thought possible.

He took her in his arms and settled her. Kissing her cheeks lightly, he said, "You must trust me. If we succeed, we live in paradise. If we fail . . . we return to hell. I'd rather be dead."

She thought about his suggestion. Hell was better than returning to the Soviet Union.

She kissed him hard on the mouth and then led him to the door. "Be careful," were her parting words.

Then he was gone, and again, like when he left before, she was alone to wonder her fate. His fate.

Again she was afraid.

26

The young men assembled in the shattered remnants of a small store had taken the name *Amabuthu* from their Xhosa language, which meant young lions, comrades, guerrillas, or soldiers. However, most of the young Amabuthu preferred the pure translation of the word: young warrior!

Patricia Gable and Ruth Mathatheta had waited for hours for the young warriors to return. When the Amabuthu came into the store, which was no more than a sorry excuse for a shanty shack, they were covered with blood and bore the wild eyes of young men who had faced horror and survived.

An animal look.

Harold Mamelodi was the leader of Amabuthu, the youthful group of warriors sworn to fight the white supremacists from their township.

Harold was tall, muscular, though he appeared skinny; his dark eyes burned with the same urgency as the wail of sirens filling the air. At sixteen, he was one of the veterans of the Amabuthu, having joined the young warriors at twelve. He had seen combat in the township, though most of the fights had been with Zulu workers. His sister had died from knobkerrie blows in an earlier riot. Harold had personally killed the assailant with his homemade assegai, a spear fashioned from a piece of metal taken from the suspension of a burned-out automobile.

He carried a thick scar across his face, another scar, this one from a white SAP officer.

Patricia knew Harold Mamelodi was one of the many angry young men in the township; young men who saw the moment as historical.

"It's what we've waited for. The moment has come to rise up and destroy the white devils. Why should we help find Loweta? He will only cow to the Afrikaners."

"He won't cow. He will try to prevent a slaughter." She was angry. Pointing outside, she said, "They are just waiting for the opportunity to turn their guns on your people. Who will stop them. You? With what? If the black population gets into this fight you will be destroyed."

"We are prepared to die."

"How noble of you. But what about the others? Do you think the bullets will find only the brave? The innocent will suffer. And, ironically, you will be playing into the hands of the White Lions. Don't you see... they want you to rise up. They have airplanes, tanks, guns, and the wealth to destroy you. The White Lions want to usurp a large portion of this nation for itself. The richest portion, and exclude the black man in the process."

"Listen to her, Harold. She speaks the truth," interrupted Ruth.

Patricia stopped talking as the wail of the sirens seemed to grow louder. She looked at Harold, and the fifteen other young men sitting in the rear of the store.

Her words seemed to have a sobering affect on the young men. "If we help you find Loweta, what's in it for us?"

She shook her head. "I can't promise you anything."

Harold watched her carefully. It was the first time he had ever been asked for help by a white person. "Do you know where they have taken Mr. Loweta?"

She shook her head. "I was unable to follow." She again recounted what happened. Her flight from her father's car; watching the man shoot her father; watching Loweta being dragged away. She told how she had slipped through the insanity engulfing the city and made her way to the house of Ruth Mathatheta, the woman who kept her father's house.

Ruth's sister Nanndi was Harold's mother. Nanndi was dead. Killed earlier that month during the craziness as Xhosa and Zulu clashed in the township.

The township, and other townships, like the country, was just one of many battlefields.

Harold could see their cause was in trouble. The black movement had mentally conditioned itself for the inevitability of a showdown with the white government. A showdown several years down the road when the Afrikaners, as he considered all whites to be Afrikaners, had shown the world apartheid would not be eliminated. But not now. Patricia was right. They weren't ready. The violence between the various factions merely served the white cause, preventing the black nations from uniting into one powerful force.

Predictable to their history, the Afrikaners had devised a plan of attack that struck with the suddenness of their historical commandos.

And they did so when the black tribes were not united, another historical strategy.

Patricia reached into her pocket and removed the notebook given her by her father. She looked fondly at the notebook. She seemed to feel his presence as her fingers opened to the first page.

"What is that?" asked Harold.

"Mr. Loweta's journal. He was intending to turn this over to the Amnesty International legation scheduled to arrive next month. He gave it to my father before we left our house. He was afraid the soldiers might get their hands on it. You should read what Mr. Loweta was planning."

Harold put out his hand. She lay the notebook in his slender palm.

Unlike most of the Amabuthu, Harold was literate. The urge to fight the whites had created a devastating effect on the young warriors' education throughout the nation. Illiteracy was high among the young children, who often chose demonstration over classrooms, especially where they were being required to learn the national language, Afrikaans. But Harold could read. Nanndi had made certain of this.

Carefully he read the first page, then the second, and as he read he recalled the author, and the white man who died trying to save the journal; a white man who had shown black Africans kindness. A commodity he had known little since birth.

Harold read the notes completely. When finished, he sat back heavily in his chair. He knew what had to be done. "We must get this to one of the embassies.

The Americans, if possible. They'll know what to do."

"What is in the notebook?" asked one of the youths.

Harold held up the notebook as though it were a weapon. Which it was. "This is Mr. Loweta's organization. His secret organization. The contacts throughout the country. Men and women who are responsible for the organization of a government in the very event of what is now happening. A government that will hold the black nations together until the insurrection is over." He smiled at the notebook. "Mr. Loweta knew this day would come. He knew a white group would try to take over the government. He wanted to be prepared so that we could stand together and not add to the confusion. Which is what the Afrikaners want."

Patricia agreed. "The more violence the blacks create will only strengthen the cause of the White Lions movement. White people will become frightened, and now that there is no army, they will support the White Lions out of fear for their own lives."

Harold thought for a long moment. "Then we know what we must do."

"What?" asked a youth. His name was Matthew Mbeki. He, too, wore the scars of battle.

"We have to find Mr. Loweta. He is the only one who can bring them all together. He is the only voice the black people will listen to right now."

"Impossible!" said Matthew. "How can we find Michael Loweta? We can't travel outside the township. The White Lions are everywhere. They have all the roads blocked. And Mr. Loweta? Where is he? He could be anywhere."

"There might be a way." said Patricia.

"What?" asked Matthew.

"I can try to find Mr. Loweta."

"And do what? Free him from the White Lions?"

"I don't know. But first he must be found. I'll cross that bridge when I get to it."

Harold looked at Patricia. "Do you have papers?"

Patricia's smile broadened into a grin. Taking off her jacket, she pulled at the seam of the lining. Reaching into the rented slot she removed two passports; a driver's license matching the names on each passport was inside.

"My father had prepared a long time ago for my being on the 'move,' as he called it. He had these made for me."

She passed around the passports and licenses. Each license was in a different name with a different city address.

Harold looked at her admiringly. "It will be very dangerous."

She thought of her father. Recalled seeing him murdered. "It's already been dangerous."

Harold looked at her with admiration. Finally, he smiled for the first time since meeting her. "You will need help in carrying all this out."

"Help? From whom? I couldn't trust anybody with this notebook."

Harold countered, "There's a man you can trust."

"What man?"

"A white man in Pietermaritzburg. He is our friend."

Patricia looked warily at Harold. "How do you know he is your friend?"

Harold grinned and reached under his shirt. He pulled out an automatic pistol. "He gave me this pistol."

27

1200.

BATTLE GROUP ZULU STATION HAD STEAMED through the night from off the east coast of the Horn of Africa. Scuttlebutt raced through the ships; groups of men spoke in low, conspiratorial voices about the new mission. There seemed to be general agreement about only one thing: This was not what they had signed on to do!

Sacrette felt the tension; he couldn't sleep, the agony was so bad. He had called his squadron commanders together to get the pulse of the fighting men and he didn't like what he found. But despite the obvious disgruntlement, the BG cruised onward, toward the place that could destroy the fighting morale of the entire United States military.

By noon the BG had reached the point where flight operations could be launched and the early stages of the mission would begin: protecting the battle group and establishing an airborne radar platform.

On the flight deck the F-14s were taking off; from the waist catapult the E-2 Hawkeye launched, lifted its

---

133

nose, and banked toward its station off the coast of South Africa. The E-2, with its electronically packed, disc-shaped rotodome, would give the BG an entire radar picture of airborne activity over a three-hundred-mile radius.

Air operations had been ongoing throughout the turnaround. Night launches and recovery had gone without any problem. The admiral had ordered the men to be kept busy around the clock. The less time to think meant the less time for more doubt to settle.

Admiral Lord despised the notion of defending the state of South Africa. However, he was a sailor. A sailor obeyed orders even when the orders were distasteful.

"Admiral?" Captain Sacrette interrupted Lord's thoughts. He was standing near the large bulletproof window on the bridge.

Sacrette motioned the admiral toward the wash of red lights emanating from the CIC.

In the CIC, Sacrette went back to the chair where he had been sitting. He had spent the better part of the morning studying the "threat" library. Tapes of the military capabilities of various nations were stored there on computer. The tape he was watching was labeled *Suid-Afrikaanse Lugmag*.

"I've been studying the tactics, equipment, and locations of the SA air force. They're a good lot. Damned good pilots. Most are veterans of the war in Namibia and Angola."

"What about numbers?"

Sacrette shrugged. "They have more aircraft than we do, but ours are better. Most are Mirages. A damned good bird. But I don't believe we'll have to face them in an air battle. Not if we knock them out while they're on the ground. Precision bombing, along with the missiles from the guided missile cruisers, should eliminate the aircraft on the ground."

Lord was silent. "President de Klerk assured the President the armed forces would not be involved."

Sacrette shook his head in disbelief. "You don't really believe that, do you? A revolution is one thing, Admiral. An invasion from a foreign country is another. I doubt the South Africans are going to sit on their butts while we come rolling in, wave after wave. At some point, their national pride will demand they get into the fight. Before that happens . . . we'll have to make certain they have nothing to fight with."

Sacrette's thoughts were the same worrisome ones that Lord had been having since receiving his orders from the CNO.

"What do you have in mind?" asked Lord.

Sacrette pointed at the map depicting the country of South Africa. "The South African air wing is divided into three commands. Strike Command. Maritime Command. Light Aircraft Command. The Strike Command is our problem. Maritime and Light Aircraft Commands are mostly heloes and transport."

"What is the capability of the Strike Command?"

Sacrette explained: "Strike Command is deployed through five fighter, bomber, and reconnaissance squadrons, and backed up with reservists in their Active Citizen Force. The fighter and bomber squadrons should be our main concentration. The fighters would be our air problem; the bombers a ground problem for our troops. All five active fighter and bomber squadrons are located on the same bases. Waterkloof and Hoedspruit."

"What about the reservists? The Active Citizen Force?"

Sacrette called off the names of their bases. "Durban. Blomfontein. Lanseria. Port Elizabeth. And again, Waterkloof, the general command headquarters."

"The ACF bases will have to be targeted."

"Yes, sir. Once we go in . . . they'll get airborne and jump into the fight."

"Six targets," Lord said matter-of-factly.

"Six targets."

Lord could sense what Sacrette was leading up to. "Which means we'll need to bring in more aircraft."

"Yes, sir. I recommend you requisition an A-7 squadron from the States."

"One squadron?"

"That'll be enough. The two Hornet squadrons could handle the situation, but we don't want to come up short. The F-14s can take care of anything that slips through the net. We can knock out their ground bases in one swift strike. Destroy them on the ground before they know what's happening."

Lord saw another problem. "I'll have to tell the CNO. He'll have to get approval from the President."

Sacrette nodded, but looked severely at the admiral. "Request that President de Klerk not be informed."

Lord shook his head. "I can't guarantee they'll approve."

"Convince them, dammit. If de Klerk gets cold feet at the wrong time . . . we could be sitting ducks. They might be waiting with fighters and ground-to-air. That'll not only slow down the mission . . . but kill a lot of my pilots. Now, goddammit, we've been pushed into this thing. The least we can do is fight the fight our way.

That's the least the South African government owes us."

Again Lord shook his head and repeated himself. "I can't guarantee you the President will not advise de Klerk."

"Then you advise the President that more Americans will die. He can explain that to the families. I won't!"

Lord's mouth tightened. He was about to lambaste Sacrette, who now stared at Lord with steely cerulean eyes. Eyes now hooded in that definitive Sacrette fashion, signaling that he was ready to strike like a cobra.

"I need you on this, Boulton." Lord's voice was soft.

Sacrette had never heard the admiral call him by his first name. "I know, sir. And I need you. We've been given a shit detail mission. *A shit de-tail mission.* I don't want to lose good men for the wrong reasons."

Lord went to the red telephone and contacted the CNO. The conversation lasted eight minutes.

Sitting back down, Lord looked at Sacrette. "The CNO will call us back."

They waited like two fathers riding out the painful wait of childbirth. Neither said anything to the other. Both men appeared resigned to looking inward.

The tension had driven Lord to the brink of his moral belief. A moral nihilist, he never saw war as being either moral or immoral. He saw war as another stage in his long and proud duty to his country.

Sacrette, on the other hand, saw war as being both moral and immoral. He had long ago learned how to deal with the two values. In war, he would be fair, but moral, unless he had to be immoral. He fought to win. Conscience be damned. He hated writing those goddammed letters to families of dead young men.

When the red phone rang the tension was thick enough to taste. The technicians looked up from their radar and surveillance scopes as the admiral leaned against the bulkhead while he talked with the CNO.

Minutes later, hanging up the phone and walking back to join Sacrette, he sat down heavily and released a long sigh.

"Well?" asked Sacrette.

"Your plan is approved."

"The A-7s?"

"They'll be dispatched immediately."

And the most important question. "What about the President? Will he advise de Klerk?"

Lord shook his head. "The attack is authorized to be a complete surprise."

Sacrette flashed his magnificent white-toothed grin. "Goddamn good news." He stood. "I better get below to the hangar deck. We've got a lot of work to do."

Sacrette walked off. Lord noticed for the first time since the mission was ordered that the CAG had the swagger of the fighter pilot again.

Then he thought of all the people who were going to die when his bombers rained the fiery hell down onto the people who claimed to have built a nation in the name of God.

"Helluva business," he whispered.

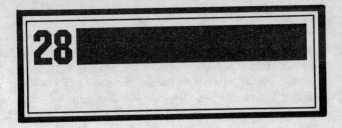

28

Mayport Naval Air Station.

LT. ALISSA BREANNE GILMORE LOOKED MORE LIKE A young movie actress than a young pilot trained to fly machines of war. She had long brown hair she wore in a bun when wearing her helmet; brown eyes that nearly melted the young pilots of her squadron; and a softness that was immediately transformed into a fighting ferocity when she climbed into the cockpit of her Vought A-7E Corsair.

She was soft and beautiful; hard and cold. "Sweet Snoots" was her call sign. That was what her daddy had called her when she was a child.

Now at twenty-five, a graduate of the naval academy, she sat in the ready room dressed in her flight suit. The unit was at full alert for the Persian Gulf crisis. She had tried to get to the Gulf but had been denied the request, along with two other female pilots. Their requests had been denied on the grounds that women could not fly in a combat situation.

Bull! She had told them. Commander Wagner, her old squadron commander, had flown a combat mission.

She had done as well as the men and was now exec of an F-18 Hornet squadron aboard the USS *Valiant*.

She looked up from her *Vogue* magazine as Lt. Commander Edward Bines entered. He was grinning from ear to ear. "Lt. Gilmore, you've been hounding my ass for three months to get into a shooting war. You're about to get your wish."

She snapped to her feet, dropping the magazine. "What's going on, sir?"

"We've been alerted for duty."

"The Gulf?" Her face was etched with anticipation.

He shook his head. "No. The carrier *Valiant*. I can't tell you any more until we have a briefing. The squadron's being notified to report for duty."

Bines left, noticing her confusion. If not the Gulf . . . then where? He did say "shooting war . . ."

Who cares, she suddenly reminded herself. Whatever was going on was better than sitting on her duff reading magazines. She went to her locker and began packing her equipment. The headquarters building was buzzing with excitement. Pilots were arriving, wearing that mask of youthful exuberance that young men—and three women—wear when learning they are about to go to war.

She thought about that. War. The terrible destructive power she could unleash from the wings and undercarriage of her aircraft was frightening to consider. People would die from the touch of her fingers. She thought about that again. And like a dedicated soldier, she placed her faith in the people who made the decision.

She would fight with all her skill. Kill if necessary— and she probably would have to. She would grieve over that someday . . . perhaps . . . in her old age when she had time and the wisdom to reflect properly.

If she survived...

She would survive.

When packed, she filed into the ready room with the other young warriors. She paused only once, asking herself again: *He did say "shooting war..."*

29

PATRICIA GABLE PEDALED AT AN EVEN PACE TOWARD the roadblock posted on the outskirts of Pietermaritzburg. Her legs throbbed from the ride; she hadn't ridden a bicycle since she was a young girl. Nearing the military checkpoint, she slowed, then alighted the bike while still moving. The bike, borrowed from Harold, was old and needed a paint job, but it was all they had.

The young soldiers wore the khaki clothes of the insurrectionists; on their shoulders was the patch of the White Lions.

"Where have you been, miss?" asked the first soldier, a handsome, dark-haired lad carrying an FN-FAL automatic rifle.

"Visiting my *oumpa*. He has a farm in the countryside."

"You shouldn't be on this road. Travel by train. It's safer. There are kaffirs on the roads. We control the trains and they are much safer."

Then she thought of a question. "Are the lines open throughout the country?"

"Yes," he replied, then added, "but only during the day. Night travel is restricted."

"Why is that?"

He smiled. "The kaffirs. They might blow up the trains. They are cowards. They won't come out during the day, but the night is different."

She took the license, then thanked the youth and began pedaling.

Kaffirs. To the Afrikaner the blacks would always be something low-life; people to be held in bondage by the harshness of apartheid.

Her legs pedaled faster. She had the address of a man in Pietermaritzburg. A friend of the Amabuthu. And she realized that she was now a member of the group, vicariously.

But what could this friend do that she couldn't do? How would he find Loweta? She didn't even know where he had been taken.

Again she thought of the danger. But, as she had told Harold, she had already seen danger.

These times were surrounded by danger.

She pedaled on, not looking back. What lay ahead was all that mattered.

PART FOUR: STAGING

30

2200.

THE MOUNTAINS OF MONTANA STOOD MAJESTICALLY
against the backdrop of a clear blue sky; a lone, white-
capped bald eagle drifted over the craggy peaks, tucked
his wings, then dove to the darkness at the base of a
valley winding along the Madison River. For an instant
the eagle was gone; reappearing, a large fish was gripped
between his mighty talons.

Home.

Sacrette sat at his desk in his office on the hangar
deck. The smells of the aircraft mingled with the scenes
on his VCR, creating a strange atmosphere. In more ways
than one he was like the eagle: a bird of prey attacking
from the sky, returning with victory in hand.

He pressed the VCR remote and ran the tape backward, stopping on the eagle. Again the bird of prey
streaked from the sky. Another victory.

Video was the greatest invention sailors at sea had
to fill the emptiness of a life that often took the men
from their families. Next to their aircraft, Sacrette and

other pilots considered the VCR the most important machine on the carrier.

Checking his watch, he was reminded of the paperwork still piled on his desk. Switching off the VCR, he was drawn to the soft rap at his door.

Commander Laura Wagner's face was creased with the telltale bruising and puffiness around the eyes often caused by high g-maneuvering. Without knowing where she had been, he could have guessed.

"How was the flight?"

"Good. The training mission went off without a hitch."

With the approach of a mission, air operations had increased. Policy dictated the fighting men and women of the navy did not just roar into battle; unless, of course, there was an immediate need for the the asset. Rather, training was stepped up until the mission began, at which time the personnel were honed razor-sharp and were merely transitioned from training targets to the real thing. This created confidence, and kept the pilots' minds busy.

Looking at her, he sensed that something was on her mind. "Is there a problem?"

She sat on the edge of his desk. "I understand my old outfit is coming aboard to join in the operation."

Sacrette nodded cautiously. "That's correct. We'll need the extra aircraft to cover all the ground targets. It'll be like old home week for you."

"Commander Edward Bines . . . is he still the exec?"

Sacrette looked into the personnel roster of the A-7 squadron. "He's still the exec."

She fluffed her short hair and stared off into the distance for a moment. She looked to Sacrette as though she were thinking about something from the past.

"Did you know that I was married to Ed Bines?"

Sacrette's face couldn't mask his surprise. "No. I wasn't aware you had been married."

"The divorce was finalized before I joined the *Valiant*. As a matter of fact, it was the divorce that prompted me to request a transfer. It became quite uncomfortable."

"Do you think that your relationship with Lt. Commander Bines will affect your performance during the mission?"

She shook her head rather emphatically. "No. I just wanted you to know. I didn't want you to be taken by surprise. As you have probably already guessed, the A-7 personnel are fully aware. I just thought you should know."

"I appreciate your honesty. And if there's any problem you know where to come."

She smiled and turned to leave. "There's something else you should know."

"What's that?"

"There's three young women pilots in the squadron. They're damn good pilots. But they're also very pretty. Very young. If you get my drift."

Sacrette frowned. He began imagining three young women surrounded by the ship's complement of sixty-five hundred men. Sixty-five hundred men who had been at sea for longer than he cared to remember.

"I'll have the CPOs remind the enlisted personnel of the rules regarding fraternization. As for the officers, I'll handle that myself."

"What will you say?" She was smirking, waiting for the bit of sage she thought would be ineffective.

"I'll remind them they are gentlemen." He was

grinning, as though he knew there was really little he could do.

"Little good that'll do."

As she went through the door, she heard the CAG mumble, "Christ."

31

Coos van Muerwe sat watching Moira at one of the many telephones in the library at Nagmaal. A skeleton crew was on duty, taking the reports from around the country. The campaign was going well.

Looking at his daughter, he found pride in the fact that she seemed tireless. A lioness with the spirit and drive of any man; in most cases he would prefer her at his side over the young men serving in his command. She, too, was a pilot. She had been the first woman in the SA air force's Active Citizens Force trained to fly Mirage jet fighters.

Hanging up the telephone, she stood and stretched, then walked over to her father. She poured a cup of coffee, asking him, "Aren't you going to get some sleep?"

His tired features formed a light smile. "I'll sleep when we have achieved our objectives."

"What's the status of the operation?"

"The security forces are doing as expected: they are sealing off the major cities, keeping a wary eye on the black population. As expected, once the campaign began, the whites of South Africa realized the delicate nature of their position. They are now watching to see what happens between our movement and the people supporting de Klerk. They'll throw in with whichever faction comes out on top."

"The President was wise not to order the security forces to attack our forces."

"He knew that would destroy the country. This is not the Boer War with Afrikaners fighting the British. The blacks are the real threat. A white versus white conflict would destroy the country. Our sources report most of the nation is viewing this as a political struggle. In time they'll understand they have no choice but to join us for their own survival."

"Have you been contacted by the military?"

"General Var der Stal and others have had emergency meetings. An emissary is enroute with a message. I suspect he'll confirm that the military will not interfere unless the blacks become involved."

Both laughed together.

Van Muerwe licked his lips at the thought of what he had in store for those whites who would sit on the fence, or stand opposing the White Lions. "Wait until they hear from Mr. bantu Loweta. Our cause will be joined in full force by the military."

A glint appeared in her eye. "What about de Klerk? Has Roos determined his location?"

"No. Not yet. But we'll find the bugger, wherever he's hiding. Our intelligence sources say he left Tuynhus for fear of his life. The fool. We won't harm him. We only want him to organize an emergency meeting of the Parliament and grant our wishes. That will give us the country we want. Problem solved."

"Has there been any suggestion of outside intervention?"

Van Muerwe nearly roared. "Who would help our government! The world stands waiting for our nation to become like the other nations in Africa: absorbed by the black population. Like Rhodesia, it would be the end of South Africa."

"Then all we have to do is wait." Her voice rang with confidence.

"Not wait. We have to consolidate our power. The military phase is nearly over. The towns and cities are secure. The military is doing nothing to interfere. What we need is the power of the people. The propaganda campaign begins tomorrow. That's when we'll begin settling the 'black problem.'"

"That will be Major Boeska's department. Where is he now? I haven't seen him since this morning."

Van Muerwe checked his watch. "He's set up a broadcast station in his home in Pietermaritzburg. He has all the radio equipment he'll need. He will begin a twenty-four-hour broadcast tomorrow morning."

Moira looked disappointed. "I have some information he wanted for the historical broadcast."

Van Muerwe knew the propaganda broadcasts would include a deluge of historical information depicting the history of the Afrikaner movement in South Africa to justification of the current policy of apartheid.

He checked his watch. "I don't want you on the highway at this hour. You can leave early in the morning."

She found this to be agreeable. "Good. I need my beauty sleep."

Van Muerwe looked fondly at his daughter. "You

could stay awake for ages and you'd still be beautiful."

She sat on his lap and for a moment they were no longer soldiers in a fight to the death; they were father and daughter.

"I pray we've made the right decision," she finally whispered in his ear.

This slight fracture in her resolve was surprising to van Muerwe. For a moment he didn't know what to say. Finally, he squeezed her tightly. "We have made the only decision we could make. History is on our side."

"History may be on our side . . . but what about the rest of the world?"

"We've stood alone before . . . we can stand alone again."

She closed her eyes and squeezed her father, and said a silent prayer that he was right.

32

1130.

IN PIETERMARITZBURG, PATRICIA GABLE HAD FOUND
the address of the man the Amabuthu claimed could be
trusted. Sitting in a restaurant across the street from the
house bearing the number scribbled onto a piece of paper, she had watched throughout the day as the house
was visited time and again by the various cars. Such
activity made her suspicious. Her first thoughts were that
the address was wrong; after rechecking the name against
the telephone directory several times she was convinced
that the address was correct.

It was nearly midnight when she saw that the street
in front of the house was finally devoid of visiting automobiles. Gathering her courage, she walked to the
front door and rang the bell. She heard a rustling behind
the door, then saw a man pull back the venetian blinds
at the large, wrought iron–covered front window.

She waited. When the door opened, nothing more
than a crack, the light bled from the inside, forming a
pallid streak across her face. Through the crack she could
see a man standing in khaki pants and white undershirt.

She almost took flight, but the door opened and the man stepped through the door. In his hand was a pistol similar to the one owned by Harold Mamelodi.

"Yes?" the deep voice asked. The voice was a baritone, and sounded as though it would belong to a singer. Or a radio announcer.

"My name is Gable. Patricia Gable. I am looking for a friend of a friend."

The man appeared to recognize the name. "Is your father Andrew Gable?" The voice asked.

"Yes. He's dead."

"I know. A great tragedy. So tell me . . . who is the friend?"

"A young man. His name is Harold. He said I could find help from his friend . . . a man named Boeska. Is Mr. Boeska around? It really is very important."

Major Cecil Boeska opened the door until he stood framed in the light coming from the living room of his home. He studied her for a long moment, then ushered her inside with a quick jerk of his hand.

Inside, she turned to a thin, frail-looking man whose voice belied his physical appearance. He appeared to be in his late forties, with balding head except for a peculiar lock of hair that was long and combed from just above his right ear, across the barren scalp of the top of his head to just above the left ear.

A ridiculous-looking sight, which nearly made her laugh. But she held her laughter; after all, this man might be her only hope.

"What is your friend's name again? His surname, please," Boeska asked. He casually allowed the pistol to slip behind his back.

"Mamelodi. Harold Mamelodi."

"That's a kaffir name," Boeska barked.

Patricia looked obstinate. "He said he was your friend."

Boeska stared at her for a long moment, then loosened. He smiled. "Quite correct. Harold and his 'chums' are friends of mine."

She pointed at the blue and white flag of the White Lions pinned to the wall. "But . . . how . . . you're a member of the White Lions."

Boeska looked at the flag. "Merely a fiction. I am no more a White Lion than was your father. Who, by the way, was a man I admired. It's a pity there aren't more like him. We worked for the same organization. Only I am not out in the open like some members."

"You're a spy for Amnesty International!" Her voice sounded gleeful, like a child receiving her first balloon.

He flushed. "I don't like the word 'spy.' It has dreadful connotations. I prefer the term 'operative of influence.'" He pointed to the kitchen. "Would you like a cup of tea?"

Patricia smiled and for the first time since the night before felt the tension begin to fall away.

She followed Boeska into the kitchen, where she stopped suddenly.

"Who is he?" she gasped.

Boeska looked nonchalantly at the dark-haired man sitting at the table. He was wearing the uniform of the White Lions.

"Don't be alarmed. He's another operative." Boeska nodded at the man. "This is Hans Diekop."

KGB Major Viktor Tragor rose and bowed slightly.

33

0800.

To the men performing maintenance on the aircraft parked in the flight hangar, the arrival of the A-7s was announced individually by the heavy *thump* overhead as the aircraft slammed onto the flight deck.

Diamonds listened to the thumps, counting until he knew the squadron had been entirely recovered. He had been in the hangar most of the night, working the men in shifts. Hard work left little time for thought. Busy hands meant busy minds.

Sacrette came out of his office, studied the long maintenance area, and called the chief over.

"Secure the A-7 squadron to the flight deck, Chief."

Farnsworth looked at the long open area of the hangar deck for a moment, as though he didn't want to address the CAG. Aircraft of all types were in various bays; mechanics were working beneath the large overhead lights.

"Do you hear me?"

Farnsworth mumbled something and started to walk off.

"Come here!" the CAG shouted.

Farnsworth stiffened, knowing years of friendship were on the line. Slowly he turned, his eyes blazing as he watched Sacrette step close. Their faces nearly touched.

"I know you dislike this situation, Chief. I don't like the situation either. But dammit, it's the order of the President that we assist."

"You're not saying anything to me that I haven't said to the men. The difference is . . . I don't have to believe that bullshit! My job is make certain they do." He jerked his thumb over his shoulder.

Sacrette studied the short, powerfully built black man for a long moment. Finally, the CAG turned, saying, "Come with me, Chief."

The two men went to Sacrette's office. From his desk the CAG took a bottle of Jack Daniel's Old Number 7. He poured two large blasts into Styrofoam cups and handed one to Diamonds.

"Fangs out!" Sacrette raised his cup as he offered the fighter pilot's battle cry for the toast.

Two old friends drank old whiskey, and as the nectar slid down their throats, each shivered when the alcohol warmed the inside of their stomachs.

Farnsworth poured another, then said, "You've got to do me a favor."

"Name it."

"You've got to get me in this mission. I don't care how you do it . . . I don't care what the job is. I can't sit on my ass while our people are fighting this battle. I've got to get in on the action."

Sacrette stared at Farnsworth for a long moment.

"If I didn't know you better...I'd say that's a racist statement on your part."

Farnsworth shook his head. Sweat beading on his bald pate trickled down his forehead. "You do know me better. But, goddammit, I can't sit on my ass while our people are fighting for freedom in Africa. I just can't do it, Thunderbolt."

There was a pleading in Farnsworth's eyes such as Sacrette had never seen before. He wasn't a man given to making promises he couldn't keep, but years of friendship did buy a few favors.

"I'll see what I can do, Chief."

Farnsworth appeared to blush. Whether from relief, or shame, since he had never asked the CAG for a favor, Sacrette wasn't sure. Nor did he care. He understood how Farnsworth felt.

"That's good enough for me."

"Now...get your ass out there and prepare to tie down those A-7s." Sacrette flashed the chief a grin.

"Aye, aye, Skipper."

Sacrette watched Farnsworth walk away; there was a distinct swagger to the chief's step as he neared the men working on the aircraft. After several loud bellows from the CPO, the maintenance crew was working with a fury they hadn't known since arriving off the coast of South Africa.

34

1015.

COLONEL VAN MUERWE WAS MORE STUNNED THAN surprised to learn that Major Cecil Boeska was at Nagmaal. Following the telephone report from the guard at the front entrance alerting the commander that his propaganda specialist was on the grounds, van Muerwe ordered Boeska to his office.

Boeska entered wearing the uniform of the White Lions. In his company was another man. Major Viktor Tragor was introduced as Hans Diekop. Tragor saluted sharply, the way Boeska had taught him.

"Hans is a new recruit. He has an extensive background in communications. He was with the Rhodesian army several years ago," said Boeska.

Van Muerwe studied Tragor closely. With over fifty thousand members in the White Lions, it was impossible for him to know each of the men and women serving the cause.

"Who did you serve with in the Rhodesian army?" asked van Muerwe.

"The Selous Scouts."

Van Muerwe's head nodded automatically. "Fine unit. Perhaps the finest special operations unit in the history of the world."

"We thought so, sir." He said "sir" in the typical British manner, making the word sound like "sah."

"What brings you to Nagmaal? I had thought you would be on the radio. Propaganda is very important at this point. Damned important."

Boeska grinned. "I thought it was time I visited the nerve center and saw for myself how things were coming along. It helps in the broadcasting. A sense of expertise and all that."

"What do you have in mind?" van Muerwe asked as he poured a cup of tea for the three men.

"Actually, sir, I was hoping to get a briefing on the progress of the movement. I'm inundated with telephone calls from throughout the country. People really do want to know what's happening. From our perspective, that is. Some government radio stations are still reporting and the information from the two sides is quite contradictory. If I knew the facts . . . I could be more effective."

Van Muerwe stepped to a large map of the country. He pointed to various cities. "The countryside is under our control. Only a few cities are in the hands of the government, mainly because we've chosen not to intimidate the local governments. By using this tactic we are, in essence, turning each city into an island. And, like it did for MacArthur, our 'island hopping' will free up more of our troops until the white population joins our ranks."

"What about the communications centers in the country?"

Van Muerwe pointed again at the map. "All major communications facilities have been destroyed. Except those we felt needed to be taken intact."

Tragor noticed the facility at Table Mountain was colored over with red. "Does that include the NASA facility at Table Mountain?"

"Especially the facility at Table Mountain. Satellite and microwave communication outside the country is nonexistent. The Table Mountain facility was the first target."

Boeska shook his head. "A shame such an elaborate facility had to be destroyed."

Tragor sensed the deep-cover KGB operative was probing.

"Not destroyed. Just deactivated. Melted, if you will."

"Melted?" asked Tragor. "How could we 'melt' the facility?"

"Modern science and technology," replied van Muerwe, who was grinning but seemed unwilling to offer more information.

Tragor and Boeska looked at each other suspiciously. Both men knew what it would take to "melt" the vast communication center overlooking Cape Town.

A catastrophic electrical failure. Only one thing could have caused such an event: Tragor nearly trembled as he realized he had found the Wolfhound!

35

1100.

THE BRIEFING ROOM WAS PACKED WITH THE AIR wing's squadron commanders and execs when Sacrette entered. He paused at the podium for a moment, examining the faces of the aviation commanders. Represented was the aircraft from the Tomcats, Hornets, Hummer, Intruder refuelers, Air Sea Rescue, Antisubmarine warfare, heloes, and the newly arrived A-7 Corsairs.

Sacrette's eyes fell onto Lt. Commander Ed Bines. He was a handsome man, perhaps even a dashing figure. On the other side of the room sat Jugs, who refused to take her eyes off Sacrette.

Sitting beside Jugs was a young female pilot. Her name tape read GILMORE. She was so pretty, he knew he'd have to keep her in the air to keep the airdales off her tail section.

Sacrette completed the operational briefing codenamed Blood River, detailing to each squadron commander their unit's responsibility. When finished he dismissed the group and started for his office.

That's when he stopped in his tracks. "I'll be damned. Look who's been invited to the party." A large grin stretched across his face as a familiar figure entered the briefing room.

"Hello, Breaker," Sacrette stuck out his hand as he approached the new arrival.

Commander John "Breaker" LeDuc shook Sacrette's hand. The commander of the SEAL special operation unit Red Cell Four had a grip like a vise. "Good to see you're not getting fat, Thunderbolt," said LeDuc, who then patted Sacrette playfully on the stomach.

Sacrette laughed. "I don't have time to get fat. These youngsters are running my ass off."

"How about a drink before we get down to business?" asked the SEAL.

Sacrette's right eyebrow rose mischievously. With Breaker's appearance, he may have solved a problem that had so far been nearly unsolvable.

"I'll buy. But first, I'll get an old friend to join us."

"Who's the friend?"

"Diamonds Farnsworth."

36

NAVY SEALs ARE AN ELITE BREED OF SAILOR; TRAIN-ing covers more than the traditional sea or land duty. SEALs are environmentally three-trained, thus the ac-ronym SEAL: Sea, Air, and Land. Training includes scuba, parachute, both military and free-fall with scuba, underwater demolitions, underwater mapping, intelli-gence gathering, weaponry, and all other critical training required to develop the world's finest fighting man.

Moreover, it is no secret that the SEALs are skilled professional killers. There's no apology for this blunt necessity. Killing is a requisite of war, and the SEALs are the forerunners of the requisite.

The Red Cell teams are SEALs, though a special unit within the infrastructure of the organization. The primary mission of the RC teams is counterterrorism, hostage rescue. The concept is simple: The RC team inserts itself into a position in which it has only one alternative—to fight to the death. At that point the ball is in the court of the enemy. The enemy must be pre-pared to kill the RC team, or suffer death at their hands.

Simple. Cold. Brutal. Reality.

Commander LeDuc was the oldest of the team members; his exec on the team was a muscular young officer, Lt. Steve Lipp. Both looked like wrestlers, and, in fact, had been wrestlers in high school and college.

The other members of RC 4 created a combination that was explosive and deadly.

The team's primary demolition specialist was a young reddish-brown–haired lad named Brooks Bollinger. Word around the fleet was that Bollinger could blow an abscessed tooth out of a sufferer's mouth without leaving so much as a headache.

Trinidad "Trini" Caisson, a Puerto Rican, was the "wet" specialist. Raised in the barrios of San Juan, he was deadly in close with the Sykes-Fairburn commando knife he wore strapped to his wrist.

Bruce "Doc" Valance was the team medic, whose heavy weapons knowledge included all the weapons of the world. His weapon of choice in the team was a SAW light machine gun.

Jesse "Bingo" Starr was the reconnaissance specialist. A black kid from Chicago, he had acquired expertise in the streets as a youth that had honed him into a man who moved like a shadow.

The RC 4 team had joined Sacrette and Farnsworth in one of the many cantinas on the carrier. Refreshments focused on several bottles of scotch LeDuc had brought aboard in his rucksack.

Pouring measured shots for each man, LeDuc raised his glass and offered a toast. "Live while you live . . . then die and be done with it."

The scotch was downed and the conversation moved to the operation.

"What time does the operation jump off?" asked LeDuc.

"The air mission will commence at twenty-four hundred. Primary ground targets will be eliminated by the F-18 squadrons and the A-7 squadron. Amphibious troops will come ashore by helo and amphibious assault vehicles. Once ashore, the marines will secure their position and prepare to move inland. The primary targets are the military installations of the South African Defense Forces. After the SADF has been neutralized we go after the White Lions. President de Klerk has assured us that once the military has been taken out of the picture the white population will be more manageable."

"What's our play on this op, Thunderbolt?" asked LeDuc.

Sacrette took out a map of the area of operation. He spread the map on the table and tapped an area north of Durban. The area was mountainous; steep walls were indicated by the tight proximity of the topographical elevation lines. A valley wound through the mountains; near the valley was a series of rivers.

"The White Lions are spread throughout the country, but their stronghold appears to be in the general area near Pietermaritzburg. Intelligence sources have confirmed the extremists are led by this man. Colonel Coos van Muerwe." Sacrette passed around a glossy photograph of the White Lions commander. The men committed the face to memory.

"Do you want him terminated with prejudice?" Lipp asked bluntly.

Sacrette shook his head. "Preferably not. President de Klerk wants him taken alive. The South African government feels that if he can be taken alive he can be persuaded to bring this thing to a halt. He's the head of the White Lions movement. Cut off the head and the body will die. But we don't want him killed. His death could result in martyrdom and the White Lions might fight to the end. You must remember . . . they are Boer descendants."

"Fanatics?" asked Bingo.

"Fanatical in their belief, certainly, but they're not cut from the same cloth as other fanatics. The White Lions are a combination of religious faith, political science, and national heritage."

"Shit," said Valance. "They sound like the PLO. Or any other terrorist organization."

Sacrette shook his head. "Not quite. The White Lions are not without a country. In fact, they now own the country. Which means they're fighting on their own real estate. Moreover, they have the support of a major portion of the civilian and military population. This is not a mission against a bunch of half-assed terrorists out to grab a few headlines for their cause. We're up against at least fifty thousand hard-core zealots with a substantial military capability that could include air and sea power."

Lipp spoke, saying, "It's my understanding the South Africans have a nuclear capability."

This revelation had a sobering effect on the group.

Sacrette nodded carefully. "Good point. The only nuclear facility we can confirm that has been developing weapons is near Pietermaritzburg. The facility is known by its only designation: Springbok Two. Intelligence from President de Klerk indicates that the facility is now in the control of the White Lions and has been rigged with tamperproof detonators."

Again the sobering effect; the SEALs drank more

Scotch, but it couldn't numb them to the grim news.

"The nuclear facility is our target?" asked LeDuc.

"That's affirmative. A specialist on nuclear detonator devices is currently en route from the Pentagon. It will be his job to defuse the detonator. Your job will be to get him to the site. In one piece," Sacrette replied. "That's your first mission. You have two primary missions."

"What's the second mission?" asked Lipp.

Sacrette tapped the map where a red X had been circled on what was a broad valley in the Drakensberg Mountains. Then he spread out several photographs the men recognized had been taken from a recon satellite.

"Nagmaal. The farm of Van Muerwe. He's using the farm as a command and control center for the overthrow. Satellite intelligence from KH-12 indicates there are heavy weapons emplacements, infantry fighting vehicles, a few tanks, with approximately two hundred ground troops in support."

LeDuc leaned and studied one of the photographs. His finger followed a long line that appeared to be a highway. The highway ended abruptly against a larger structure. "What is this? A road?"

Sacrette shook his head. "That was my thought at first." He pointed to a triangular-shaped image on the edge of a road. "That triangle is a tetrahed on. A wind-direction indicator for aircraft."

"An airstrip," LeDuc said thoughtfully. "He must be using the larger structure as a hangar. Does he have aircraft inside the structure?"

Sacrette shrugged. "That'll be another task you'll have to perform. Find out what's inside the building. It looks like a barn but I'll wager there's more than tractors and milking machines inside."

LeDuc leaned back; he looked warily at Sacrette. "Just how do you expect us to get inside this place? Which, in my opinion, is a fortress. Walk through the front gate?"

Sacrette grinned. "Something like that."

Bingo rolled up his sleeve, revealing a muscular forearm. On his wrist was the tattoo of the SEALs. Looking at the other RC 4 members, he raised an eyebrow as he said, "I know these guys could pass for White Lions . . . but I'm going to have a helluva time convincing those characters I'm a descendant of Boers."

Soft laughter rippled through the group. Farnsworth seemed equally curious as to the answer.

"With style and panache . . . style and panache." Sacrette raised his glass to the SEALs and drained the scotch.

"What have you got in mind, Thunderbolt?" Farnsworth asked dubiously.

Sacrette flashed a grin. Then he explained. When he had finished, the others merely gasped. Especially Farnsworth and Bingo.

The two black men looked at each other as though they thought the CAG had lost his senses.

37

LT. COMMANDER WAGNER WAS SITTING AT HER DESK
when she heard the knock at her door. She stiffened. A
knock at the door, in many ways, was like a signature,
or a footprint. Recognizable if done a certain way, and
heard often enough to become familiar. The musical rap
was familiar. One she had heard many times before.

"Come in, Ed," she said aloud.

Lt. Commander Ed Bines was wearing his flight suit.
He smiled sheepishly, then seemed to gather his com-
posure. "Can we talk?"

She stared a hole through her former husband.
"What's there to talk about?"

He shrugged. "The mission. What else?"

Jugs dropped her pen on the report she was filing
on the morning's flight operations and leaned back in her
seat. Her eyes darted to a chair.

"What about the mission?"

Jugs had learned that when you've flown one particular type of airplane long enough you come to know and
anticipate the aircraft. The aircraft becomes comfortable,

predictable. She had come to realize that people were the same way. Men especially. And especially a man who had been her husband. His arrival in her office was predictable, as was the arrogant way he sat in the chair. He seemed to be waiting for her to start the conversation.

"Well?" she prompted. "What about the mission?"

"It's my understanding you'll be leading the 'strike' phase of the operation."

"That's correct. Captain Sacrette will lead the air defense and intercept." She paused for a moment, then shot to the heart of what she suspected was his reason for coming to her office. "Do you still have a problem with being under the command of a woman?"

Bines's cheshire grin evaporated, replaced by a sullen mask. "This is my squadran's first combat action. I thought it would be appropriate if I led my squadron. I am the squadron commander."

Jugs remained motionless as she spoke. "Captain Sacrette has assigned the targets to the specific sortie. He wants the F-18s and A-7s intermingled. I agree. That will give us a broader base of weaponry on the targets. Your Walleye and Maverick 'smart' bombs mixed with our Maverick and laser-guided bombs will give us an overlapping punch. We can minimize collateral damage. That's why Captain Sacrette requested another bomber squadron. The more 'smart' ordinance we can deploy, the less chance of destroying nonessential targets."

Bines's face tightened. "You never quit, do you?"

"Quit what!" she snapped back.

"Playing the role. Playing the goddammed role of the modern-day Joan of Arc."

Joan of Arc. Damn him. That was what he called her when they were married. That and Iron Ass.

She started to climb over the desk but then decided to remain calm, allowing her facial features to soften before she responded. Command was more than being able to chew ass . . . it included being calm and in control regardless of the situation.

Or the personal anger.

"Lt. Commander . . . I am no longer your wife. I am the exec of this battle group's air wing. You have been given an order by the CAG . . . who expects you to carry out the order with disregard for your personal feelings. If you have a problem with the plan of this operation, I suggest you speak with the CAG. He's the authority on this matter."

She picked up her pen and resumed writing. After several seconds he was still in his chair. Saying nothing. Fuming.

She looked up, and said to him what she had wanted to say since the day she returned to their apartment and found his clothes had been packed and moved out. Along with him.

"Ed . . . you're dismissed!"

38

IN THE SECURED HOLDING CELL BENEATH THE FIRST
level of the bombproof barn serving as a hangar, Jan Roos
turned the handle of the *sjambok* in his meaty palms.
Fiendishly, he extended the harsh tip to the soft tissue
beneath the chin of Michael Loweta, lifting slightly so
as to raise Loweta's face to his. The face was unmarked.
The technique used by Roos was a different sort of per-
suasion.

The bare skin of the body had not been touched,
but the constant whipping through the clothes worn by
Loweta had bruised and stung his body repeatedly. The
mind was now pliable. Easily persuaded by the threat of
another beating.

Roos picked up the telephone and dialed the main
house.

"The kaffir is ready. The tape is ready, sir," he
said, his voice gravelly, as though he spoke while simultaneously trying to clear his throat.

Roos listened to the instructions from Van Muerwe.
Hanging up the telephone, Roos reached to a tape re-

corder on the table. He popped out a cassette and dropped the cassette into his pocket.

An evil smile cast toward Loweta, who sat motionless, feeling the shame of his actions.

Roos went to the elevator and made the short ride to the surface.

Loweta's face was twisted with that special mixture of anger and pain a man feels when he has been forced to do something against his will.

He felt as though he had betrayed his people. Soon, if these men had their way, he would betray his people.

39

1215.

WHILE BOESKA DISCUSSED THE UPCOMING PROPA-
ganda campaign with van Muerwe, Tragor slipped
through the front door and roamed the grounds. The first
maxim of the intelligence officer is to know when he is
being observed; he took a broken course through the
farm, acting as though he were examining the gun place-
ments. Noting he was not being observed, he gradually
drifted toward the largest structure on the farm.

At the front of the barn he encountered two security
guards. Identification wasn't requested. Admittance was
denied, however, by the sign that read: AUTHORIZED
PERSONNEL ONLY!

Strolling to the side of the barn, he could see that
it was impregnable. He was mentally committing the
barn to his memory, noting the thickness of the heavy
doors, the oversize depth of the concrete slab the barn
was built on. There were no power joints at the outside
of the building, suggesting that the structure was elec-
trically independent.

Of peculiar interest was the road running out from

the barn. The composite wasn't concrete, which might give away its purpose from the air. Rather, van Muerwe had constructed the road from a special mixture of blacktop and crushed rock. A thin layer of dirt coated the road, which he now knew was a runway.

His suspicions might have been confirmed at that point, when he suddenly saw something that made his stomach tighten. A face in a photograph shown him at the First Directorate headquarters.

"Demlov," he whispered.

Sergei Demlov was coming from the swimming pool at the rear of the main house. A towel was slung over his bronze shoulders; he wore a skimpy bathing suit. His blond hair was lighter now after only a few days in the hot African sun.

He looked like one of the White Lions.

Nearing the pilot, Tragor's impulse was to make a quick move, step inside Demlov's stride and drive the heel of his hand into the point of Demlov's chin. The force of the blow would kill the traitor. The move would, no doubt, cost Tragor his life. No, he told himself. Killing the pilot would only solve the problem temporarily. Van Muerwe was a resourceful enemy. With Demlov dead, the Afrikaner would be forced to learn to fly the aircraft himself. If he wasn't already learning. At least, he would learn if necessary. Such a prize could not be allowed to sit idle for a technical problem that could be solved.

Nearing Demlov, he had to be certain it was the Soviet defector. Tragor spoke in a pleasant Afrikaner-accented voice. "Good afternoon."

Demlov looked at him with surprise. He seemed to recognize Tragor, which the KGB spy knew was impossible. But Russians were innately suspicious; the conditioning of living in the Soviet Union had forced this instinct upon all of them.

Demlov covered his midsection with his towel. "You're not authorized in this area."

Tragor smiled inwardly. The accent was thick, positively Russian. Only the KGB operatives sent to the West had years of language training required to filter out the accent of the Russian language.

"My apologies. It is such a pleasant day . . . and I've been cooped up all night. The fresh air from a stroll seemed to be the right prescription."

Demlov grunted, then said something under his breath as he walked away.

Tragor went back to the main house. He found Boeska with van Muerwe and a young woman. Boeska was rubbing his chin slightly, a prearranged signal between the two should either spot trouble. Boeska's eyes drifted to the woman.

"Moira will accompany you to your broadcasting center. I have given her a tape I wish broadcast tonight. I want her to announce the tape." The pride on the fighter commander's face was obvious.

Tragor said nothing. "The pleasure of such delightful company would be most appreciated."

Moira's left eyebrow rose slightly. She studied Tragor for a moment; the KGB operative sensed she was not displeased by what she saw.

Tragor was pleased as well. The woman was not only beautiful—she was valuable.

Tragor shook hands with Moira. The trio was preparing to leave when van Muerwe suddenly remembered something important. "One moment. There is another matter to be attended to." Van Muerwe pressed a button and spoke over the intercom to his secretary: "Bring him in."

Seconds later Jan Roos came through the door.

Tragor nearly choked at seeing Roos, whom he recognized. As Resident of the Illegals operation, he knew all the faces of high-level Special Branch personnel. His only hope was that the henchman didn't know his identity.

The question was answered within seconds as Roos hurried past Tragor. The two men's eyes met for just a moment.

There was no recognition.

Van Muerwe took the cassette from Roos. "Our guest is going to perform a service for the cause. You will take this tape to your broadcasting center in Pietermaritzburg. I want the tape played every hour on the hour. Roos will accompany you to report back with the intelligence evaluation after he contacts our various agents throughout the country."

"What tape is this, Colonel?" Boeska asked.

"A plea from the kaffir Michael Loweta urging the black population to rise up and destroy the white South Africans!"

Boeska looked astonished. "You want to play such a tape over our broadcast! That's not wise, Colonel. Not wise."

Van Muerwe stiffened at having his judgment questioned. "Before you play the tape, you will announce that the tape was intercepted by our people. Stipulate that the tape was taken from a courier for the ANC. The tape was en route to Zimbabwe to be played over the Zimbabwe national radio."

Boeska knew the ANC transmitted into South Africa hourly. Millions of blacks received news of the outside world from the broadcast station located in Baitbridge on the South African border.

"How *did* you acquire the tape?" asked Boeska.

A leer cut across van Muerwe's features. "Mr. Loweta is a personal house guest." He arrogantly lifted his head in the direction of the barn.

"Isn't that dangerous?" asked Tragor.

The leer deepened into a sinister glare that made Tragor's skin crawl.

"The movement must consider all contingencies— both current and future. We will have to teach the kaffir a lesson soon enough, after the government grants our nation-state and the blacks have their country. We may as well deal with them now—while we have the resolve—and the means."

Tragor understood the meaning. He saw through the thin facade of white survival. Of white independence. He saw clearly the ultimate goal of the White Lions.

If the white population feared a black uprising was eminent, the military, neutral this far, would join with van Muerwe. Total war would follow. War directed to the carefully orchestrated concentrations of black Africans van Muerwe knew would serve as holding pens: the townships.

And the White Lions had the perfect morale-destroying, frightening weapon to begin the slaughter: a particle beam weapon, spewing death and fear from the Wolfhound!

PART FIVE: SPRINGBOK TWO

40

PATRICIA GABLE HAD SHIVERED AT THE SIGHT OF
Roos. She recognized the murderer of her father. The
only consolation was knowing that Loweta was somewhere close. At the farm, Tragor had whispered to her
after they had returned to Boeska's house, which was
more of a broadcasting center than a home.

Banks of electronic equipment lined the wall and a
small soundproof broadcasting booth was stationed in the
center of the front part of the house. Tragor could see
where walls had been removed, probably covertly, in the
days prior to the beginning of the insurrection to prevent
the government from knowing about its existence. The
station was now playing nonstop propaganda interspersed
with occasional soft music.

Van Muerwe's tape was played over the air, introduced first by Moira, who spoke of her father as though
talking about God.

Roos was at a telephone, contacting various agents
throughout the country, instructing them on what to do
following the airing of the Loweta call to arms.

Patricia stared contemptuously at the assassin, who was the head of the Security Commando.

"You must control your emotions, my dear," Tragor whispered to her as he handed her a cup of tea.

Patricia studied his face. She had given the Russian little thought since meeting him the night before. During the day, while alone at the home of Boeska, she began thinking about the man who was, no doubt, an infiltrator of the White Lions, like Boeska.

Yet Tragor seemed different. He wasn't a follower. He was a leader; that was obvious in the way he carried himself.

"Leader of what?" she asked herself. There was nothing to lead. Perhaps he was a spy for the government, sent to monitor the situation for the government. Boeska as well.

If so, why wasn't Roos aware of their identities? The former Special Branch operative would know the identities of all the SB agents working for the government, especially some one as schooled as Tragor appeared.

No. He doesn't work for the government. If not, then who?

Tension now threaded through the room as Moira completed her phase of the broadcast.

Roos reached into his pocket and started toward the cassette player.

"I'll take the cassette, Mr. Roos." Tragor's voice was the only sound in the booth.

Roos turned to see Tragor standing at the small door. In his hand was an automatic pistol.

"You bastard! Are you insane?" roared the assassin.

"Not quite. But if you think I'm going to let you play that tape and spill millions of black Africans into this little party of yours . . . you're sadly mistaken. Give me the tape." Tragor extended his free hand.

Roos's facial muscles twitched beneath the skin. "Who are you?"

Tragor smiled politely. "The man who is going to shoot a hole through your forehead if my instructions are not followed."

In the next instant the confusion that followed was prompted by a combination of bravado, loyalty, and contempt for betrayal.

Moira Prouse's hand had slowly eased to the tiny pocket in her bush jacket. Gripping a small .25-caliber pistol, her hand rode carefully onto her lap.

"Tragor!" shouted Boeska, who leapt between the woman and the Russian.

Moira's finger closed around the trigger. The bullet from her pistol tore a small hole through the left eye of Boeska, pitching the man's body toward Roos, whose hand was moving to the pistol holstered on his belt.

Tragor fired once, then fired the second shot from the Browning 9mm automatic pistol given to him by the woman in Durban.

The first bullet tore through the side of Moira's brain, exited beneath the opposite ear, spewing a trail of bluish-gray brain matter against the glass of the sealed room.

Roos was hit in the throat, which he clutched while falling to his knees, knowing his life would soon be gone.

He tried to yell, but nothing issued but a garbled realization of who Tragor was. "K.G.B.," he gurgled.

Roos fell forward; smoke wafted through the enclosed room, creating an eerie scene that shook Patricia Gable to the core.

A sickening wave of nausea raced through her system as she looked at the three dead people who only an instant before had been animate: talking, moving, breathing.

She wanted to run, but there was no strength in her legs.

She wanted to scream but the cotton dryness in her mouth could not bring forth a sound.

She sat still; trembling, she watched the barrel of the pistol and studied the hole in the barrel, waiting for death to spew forth.

Nothing happened. The barrel lowered to Tragor's side, then disappeared into a shoulder holster beneath his jacket, which was unbuttoned to his waist.

"Who are you?" she asked weakly.

"I'm a friend."

"American?"

He shook his head. "My nationality doesn't matter."

"But you are not South African." It wasn't a question.

Tragor rocked back on his heels. "I have been sent here to recover a piece of property belonging to my government. A deadly weapon the White Lions are using against the opposition and, I suspect, will be using against the blacks very shortly."

"What kind of weapon?"

"An aircraft. A very sophisticated aircraft. An aircraft I must recover or destroy."

"Can you recover the aircraft?"

He shook his head. "That's doubtful. There's too much security around the aircraft."

"Then how can you destroy it?"

"There's a way. It'll be very dangerous. But I know a way. I'll need your help."

"Why should I help?"

Tragor took the cassette from beside the body of Roos. Holding up the cassette, he said, "I know where you can find your friend Loweta."

She looked at him for a long moment. "How can I help?"

41

SACRETTE STOOD IN THE PRY-FLY TOWER, THE ROOST of the air boss—the man who oversees flight operations during launch and recovery. He was watching the insertion of the first piece of equipment into Operation Blood River.

On the flight deck, locked into shuttle tension, an E-2 Hawkeye was running up the engines to launch revolution. The turboprops spewed tiny tornadoes of vortices against the blast deflector shield, protecting the launch crew from the tremendous backwash.

On the deck the men wearing multicolored shirts depicting their particular jobs were scrambling about, readying for the ultimate test of the workmanship: the crossbowlike firing of the Hawkeye from the cat.

Steam drifted up in the cat tracks as the launch officer built up the needed pressure to insure proper launch. Weight and aircraft design determined what pressure was used. Too much and the aircraft would be torn to pieces along the run; too little and the aircraft would pitch over the bow to the darkness of the sea.

"Launch the Hawkeye when ready," the air boss ordered.

On the deck, a launch officer was kneeling beneath a wing of the AWAC aircraft. He was making a final careful study: ailerons set to the right angle; launch bar joined properly to the shuttlecock; even the vibration in the air, sensing the RPM's building to the right setting. When all was ready, the officer leaned in the direction of the bow and pointed two fingers toward the blackness beyond the bow.

An instant later the cat fired, driving the Hawkeye along the track; beneath the wing, the launch officer felt the wing sweep knifelike by his head, missing him by only inches.

With a thunderous *whoosh!* the Hawkeye bolted off the deck, dipped, then rose, banked sharply, and disappeared into the night.

The airborne early warning electronic platform was en route to its station off the coast of South Africa. From there the Hawkeye could monitor all airborne traffic inside and out of South Africa for a three-hundred-mile radius.

Sacrette patted the air boss on the shoulder, "Good job, Perry." Commander Perry Zimbleman didn't pay any attention to the compliment; he was busy with the next launch, an F-14 Tomcat.

Leaving the pry-fly tower, Sacrette made his way to his office. On the lower level, the massive hangar deck was packed with aircraft undergoing final preparations prior to launch into the operation.

At the weapons elevator, racks of bombs were being examined, making certain fuses were properly on safe; electronics technicians were giving the electronically guided "smart" weapons a thorough inspection. Large gurneys contained boxes filled with the 20mm cannon ammunition the fighters would carry for their M-61 Vulcan machine cannons.

The taste of war was in the air. The nervous tension the men felt earlier was gone, replaced by the urgency of doing their duty.

Sitting in the cockpit of her A-7, which was on the deck for landing gear repair, Lt. j.g. Alissa Gilmore was wearing her flight suit as she checked the cockpit instrumentation. Using a spot on another aircraft, she turned on the laser targeting system and used the mark as a zeroing point to assure that the equipment was working with pinpoint accuracy.

"I could split hairs with it," she said aloud.

"You may have to," a voice from below countered.

Looking down, Alissa saw Jugs standing at the leading edge of the wings, which were folded back to conserve space on the cramped deck.

"Are you nervous?" asked Jugs.

Alissa shrugged. "Certainly. Are you?"

"I'm always nervous. It keeps me alert—and that's what keeps you alive."

Alissa looked around. "I've never seen anything like this before. It's orchestrated confusion."

"Good analogy." She motioned her down. "Come on. I'll buy you a cup of coffee."

The two pilots went to Jugs's office. The exec poured coffee, then sat down in her chair. "I've made some changes. I want you flying my dash two in the operation. You can look at the bombing schedule and make any necessary changes."

Alissa liked the idea of two women flying wing-towing

into combat. But she sensed there might be another reason. "You're not playing the mother role, are you?"

Jugs shrugged. "Maybe I am. That's my option. It has nothing to do with your capability. I just want to be certain I've got a good wingman—wingwoman—flying with me."

Sensing there might be more to this conversation than the discussion of tactics, Alissa asked pointedly, "Is there something on your mind?"

Jugs studied the cup for a moment as though gazing into a crystal ball. Finally, she stared straight into Alissa's eyes. "How would you like to join this squadron? Fly Hornets instead of Crusaders?"

Alissa nearly gasped. "I don't believe what I've just heard. Of course I would."

Jugs expanded on the proposition. "More and more women are going to have the opportunity to do some role changing in the next few months. I believe women are going to have their place in the war in the Gulf. Not many, but it will advance the argument that could change our role in the military of the future. I want to be ready for that change. A woman is now the captain of a guided missile cruiser in the Gulf; women are near the front lines in Saudi Arabia. I believe women pilots will one day have a substantial role in carrier operations."

"Sounds like you have visions of becoming the CAG."

"I may well become a CAG. If I'm good enough. I don't apologize for having ambition. I've earned what I have. I want more than a retirement certificate. I want to help effect change. But that means the right people have to be brought on board. Have you been to Top Gun?"

She shook her head. "My application was disapproved."

"Resubmit your application when you return stateside. After Top Gun apply for Hornet training. When you complete that training you'll be ready to fly in a battle group."

"Aren't you forgetting something?"

"What?"

"This mission. You make it sound as though I'm guaranteed to survive."

Jugs smiled softly. "You'll survive."

"I wish I were as sure as you."

"You have to be sure. Otherwise, you wouldn't be able to climb into that cockpit in a few hours."

"Will that be the test?"

"That's the test. Short and simple. No multiple choice or essay questions. Just a simple act on your part. Can you do it?"

Alissa's jaw tightened. "I can do it."

42

1800.

DARKNESS WAS SETTLING OVER THE INDIAN OCEAN; in the distance the sun was nothing more than a slightly glowing reminder. On the flight deck, seven men moved about through the veiled darkness with ease, catlike and quiet. Each man carried a heavy rucksack and a variety of weapons from pistols to M-16s, crossbows to the SAW.

The Red Cell team was preparing to go into war.

An SH-60 Seahawk helo sat warming its engines. Sacrette stood by the opened door of the fuselage, watching the men load their equipment.

"Diamonds, you have another passenger." Sacrette whipped his thumb toward the island. Walking from the massive superstructure was a small figure.

"Who in the hell is that?" asked the CPO.

"The reason you're along on this mission. The SEALs have their job . . . you have yours. That's the specialist who'll be deactivating the nuclear devices. You're the baby-sitter. Don't let anything happen to him."

Lt. Commander Hamilton Bird was a fourth-generation naval officer from Massachusetts. He was also an expert on nuclear detonation devices. He certainly didn't look like a fighting man.

He was short, rail-thin with a pinched face. His large eyes gave him the presentation of a man starving to death. But he was one of the best men at doing his job, and had eagerly volunteered for the mission. He was flown to the carrier from the Pentagon where he was stationed with the Chief of Naval Operations.

Sacrette gathered the men and introduced the SEALs to Bird. He appeared like a bee-bee in a boxcar alongside the hulking warriors.

"Take good care of this man, Chief. He's more important than you," Sacrette said, somewhat tongue-in-cheek.

"I'll stick him in my pocket if things get tense," chided the chief.

Bird said nothing. He climbed into the helo with the others, except Diamonds and Breaker, who were still with Sacrette.

"You know your job, gentlemen. It's imperative that you succeed. Until we hear from you . . . we won't light the candle from this end. You have to deactivate that nuclear facility."

"Consider it done," said Breaker, who extended his hand to Sacrette. "We'll cool down the nuclear facility, then get on the road to the next site."

Sacrette thought about the second phase of their two-pronged mission. "I wish you the best of luck."

The men saluted in the twilight. Minutes later, like a giant dragonfly, the helo lifted off the deck and raced into the darkness.

Operation Blood River was officially off the ground.

43

IN THE CIC, LORD WAS WATCHING ONE OF THE FILMS from the threat library depicting SA fighters in air operations against Cuban pilots in the war in Namibia. "They're damned good," he said softly.

"We're damned better," a voice countered over his shoulder.

Lord turned to see Sacrette coming into the CIC. He was dressed in his flight suit and speed jeans.

"The SEALs are en route," reported the CAG.

Lord pointed his finger at a young technician sitting at an instrument console. The technician pressed a single button. On the wall, a clock began to run. Like a staff of surgeons in the operating room, the staff in the CIC would watch the clock from time to time, keeping track of the time involved with the patient. In this case . . . a combat operation.

"Christ," said Lord. "I'll be glad when this damn operation is over."

"You and every man in this battle group. The men

are working well together, but there's a lot on their minds."

"There should be. But what makes me proud is the stand they're taking. Almost to the man. Black and white. Damn. Thirty years ago you'd have seen a totally different picture."

"Times change."

"Yes. It's unfortunate that the South Africans can't understand that keen fact. They refuse to change—now they will be forced to change. When this is over—their country will never be the same."

Sacrette looked at the film on the threat library. "Damn shameful waste of good aircraft. I just hope the pilots stay on the ground. I'd hate to waste a lot of good pilots."

Lord watched the threat library. An aerial dogfight was under way between a Mirage and a Soviet-built Foxbat with Cuban markings. The Foxbat disintegrated as a rocket found its mark from the Mirage.

In the next sequence of footage the camera crew was filming the victorious pilot. A close-up of his face made Lord comment wryly, "That's one fight I wish the Cubans had won."

Sacrette nodded. "Yeah. It would make life a lot simpler right now."

From the screen burned the smiling, bronzed face of Colonel Coos van Muerwe.

"I'll send him your regards if we meet," said Sacrette.

"He's good."

"I'm better!"

44

"WHAT DO YOU MEAN SHE'S IN GOOD HANDS? PUT HER on the telephone." Van Muerwe listened angrily as the voice reported what he was steadily realizing was the worse nightmare of his life. "Ransom! What bloody ransom are you talking about, you bastard!"

From Pietermaritzburg, Viktor Tragor leaned back in the chair and allowed the man to seethe. "You have stolen an airplane belonging to my government. I have stolen a woman belonging to you. I suggest we arrange a swap. Our plane for your daughter."

"You bloody Russian bastard. I'll have your balls for this treachery!"

Tragor countered: "Don't threaten me, Colonel. I might cut off your daughter's ears and send them to you as a means of proving my determination."

"You bastard! You wouldn't dare."

"I'm KGB . . . and I'm running out of time. I want my country's aircraft."

Van Muerwe snorted. "What do you suggest I do . . .

put the bloody plane on a bloody lorry and drive it over to you?''

"No. I expect you to have Demlov fly the aircraft to Zimbabwe. The Soviet air attaché in Harare will know what to do with the Wolfhound."

"Demlov! Preposterous. That bloody mercenary wouldn't agree to such a notion. Your people will boil him in oil if they get their hands on him. He's a mercenary . . . a traitor . . . but he's not a fool."

"Then there's only one alternative."

"Which is?"

"The Wolfhound must be destroyed."

There was a long pause on the other end as Tragor waited to hear the response. "Destroy the Wolfhound? I can't destroy the Wolfhound!"

"I realize your predicament. But I also have a solution. Listen very carefully." Tragor explained his plan.

Van Muerwe listened incredulously. "This is not a decision I can make on my own."

"Don't be ridiculous. It's a decision only you can make. What are you suggesting, discussing this with your co-conspirators? They would never agree to such an arrangement. You have to do this without their knowledge."

"Then what?"

"I give you back your daughter. You return to establishing your white Afrikaner homeland, and I'll return to my business."

"What if I don't agree? My daughter is a soldier. She's prepared to die for her country."

"I've considered the possibility that you might say those very words. But she will not die as a soldier."

"What do you mean?"

"If the aircraft is not destroyed—I've been ordered to deliver your daughter to some of our young comrades in the Soweto township. I'm sure you can figure out her fate. A beautiful white-skinned, blondhaired White Lioness in the hands of those gentlemen from the ANC."

Tragor knew he was playing the last card in his deck. He had planned to use the daughter to get to the Wolfhound, but what he had not anticipated was having to kill the woman. He was now running on bluff and bluster.

And the love of a father for his daughter.

Van Muerwe couldn't think. He simultaneously saw images of the aircraft burning—and his lovely daughter being violated.

In the end, he capitulated. "Tell me what you want me to do."

Tragor gave van Muerwe his precise instructions. When finished, he picked up one of the portable communicators carried by the White Lions. "Do you have a portable communicator?"

"Of course."

"Good. After the aircraft has been destroyed I'll contact you on the following frequency. I'll tell you where to make the exchange for your daughter. And one other thing: When you come—bring Michael Loweta with you. If I don't see him, the arrangement is concluded. Do I make myself clear?"

"Quite clear."

Tragor hung up. He looked at Patricia. "We have to leave immediately. Van Muerwe may have sent his men. We'll leave Boeska and Roos, but we'll have to dispose of the woman."

Tragor picked the woman up from the chair and

carried her to Boeska's bedroom. He was careful not to leave a trail of blood. In the bedroom he went into the closet and opened a panel that led to a secret room similar to the one at Rhoda Zweel's apartment.

He laid the body on the floor, then stripped off her uniform. He handed the uniform to Patricia. "Put this on."

She looked stunned.

"Put it on," he snapped.

While she dressed, Tragor searched through the room until he found what he was looking for. A long wooden box with leather carrying straps was beneath several piles of blankets.

When Patricia was dressed he took the box and walked back to the front room. He took one final look around to be certain there was no trail.

"Come. We have to hurry."

45

THE SH-60B SEAHAWK HAS A CRUISING SPEED OF 167 mph, which isn't especially fast in light of most aircraft; however, when the aircraft is flying at night, at ten feet above the ground through mountains, the tendency among the passengers is to sit silently, their asses sucking the nylon off the webbed seats.

A more harrowing experience can't be imagined, as Bird was learning on this, his first ever military insert.

"Nothing to worry about, Commander," said Diamonds, who was wearing a pair of Starlight night-vision goggles. "These guys do this all the time. Besides, if something goes wrong—you'll never know it."

Bird leaned and yelled over the howl of the engine. "That's comforting to know, Chief. Very comforting. It's rather like defusing a nuclear device—if you fuck up, you'll never know."

Bird's mouth stretched into a grin, and Farnsworth felt his ass suck tighter.

"Ballsy bastard," the chief told himself. He looked outside. The Drakensberg Mountains raced by in nothing more than a blur. Looking around he saw the SEALs were content with the situation. Having been a former SEAL, Diamonds knew their mind-set at this moment. They weren't thinking about dying.

They were thinking about killing.

In the front, the pilot was training his eyes on the forward terrain, not the instruments. His movements were subtle as the helo rose to avoid an obstacle, then lowered to get back into the ground effect from riding so close to the terrain.

Below, a river snaked lazily through the mountains. Looking through the opened door, Bird recognized the river that served as a battle cry for the South Africans.

"The Blood River," said Bird, pointing to the valley where Retief's party was murdered.

"Helluva name for a river," said Diamonds.

"The South Africans are a historically oriented people, Chief. You shouldn't be offended by the way they feel about black people."

"That's bullshit! Sir! I am offended."

Bird shook his head. "You're missing my point."

"What is your point? Sir!"

"Don't be offended by me, either. I just want you to understand what kind of people you're dealing with. This is not the South, and the tactics of the Civil Rights movement can't be used. In the Civil Rights movement, the white majority supported the movement. Otherwise, the movement could not have succeeded. Here, the whites are the minority. Imagine the South, with the minority black population in control and the white population subservient."

"That's a ridiculous concept."

"Of course it's ridiculous. A minority ruling over a

majority. But that's what you have in South Africa. A ridiculous situation. With frightened people in control. Throughout their lives they have been raised to believe black people are less than human. They have been fed the history of the slaughters and golden days of the Afrikaner, much like we're raised on sports heroes. In a way, they're to be pitied."

"I don't pity the South Africans."

"Of course you don't. But take it one step further and maybe you can at least understand them."

"What step?"

"Put yourself in their shoes. What would you do?"

"I don't have to put myself in their shoes. I know what's right. I know what's wrong."

"Certainly. You're fortunate. You risk nothing but your life. The Afrikaners fear they are risking their existence. The South Africans base their title on the assumption that they were the first inhabitants of the southern tip of Africa."

"Were they?"

"It depends on what evidence you believe. That's why there are Homelands. The white South Africans conceded that those areas were inhabited by black tribes on their arrival. All remaining territory they claim for themselves based on discovery and settlement."

"It's like the American West."

"In some ways. With one major difference."

"What's that?"

"The Indians were soon in the minority. They became vastly outnumbered. In South Africa, it's the opposite. But the white South Africans still have the power. The wealth. The means to turn the wealth into more power. The Indians had nothing but their culture."

"Where does it all end?"

Bird grinned. "Here. Now. With this insurrection, South Africa will never be the same. And the President wouldn't have gotten us into this mess if he weren't certain that changes would come. It's a new day dawning for South Africa. The white South Africans will have to learn to trust the blacks."

"That'll be hard."

"Why?"

Diamonds stared Bird straight in the eye. "How do you trust someone you don't believe exists except as a subhuman?"

Bird nodded sympathetically. "That will be their first task. To learn to accept the black majority as equals."

Neither men said anything else for the rest of the ride to the insertion point.

The helo settled onto an open area near a road. The SEALs and Farnsworth climbed out. The roar of the Seahawk's rotors was barely audible as the whisper mode silenced the engines to a low purr.

Watching the helo depart, Farnsworth was nearly overwhelmed by a sudden realization: He was now standing in Africa, his ancestral homeland!

"Man," he said aloud. "Mother Africa."

LeDuc clapped him lightly on the back, "Welcome home, Chief. Now, let's go help take it back."

Silently, the commando force slipped from the brush-covered veld to the gravel road, where they began a steady jog toward Springbok Two.

Twice the age of most of the SEALs, Farnsworth

felt stronger, with each step as though the taste of the African night had supercharged his body with the spirit and strength of the great Zulu warriors who had once roamed these hills as kings.

46

2130.

THE LIGHTS FROM SPRINGBOK TWO BURNED IN-
tensely against the night; a high, ribbon wire-topped
fence formed a perfect square around the facility. Pho-
toelectric lights mounted every fifty feet lit up the
grounds outside the facility; the same type of lights
turned inward lit up the interior.

From a hillock overlooking the facility, Farnsworth
lay studying the layout through his Starlight binoculars.
LeDuc lay at his side, doing the same.

"There's the main entrance," said LeDuc.

A guardhouse stood in front of a gate that appeared
locked and chained. Two guards dressed in White Lions
uniforms were sitting inside the guardhouse.

"They're playing cards," whispered LeDuc.

"Not all of them. Look who's watching the front
door."

At the front of the door stood a large dog.

"That's a bull mastiff," said Farnsworth. "One helluva ass-eating dog."

They could see the dog suddenly stick its nose up

and check the wind. The dog began pacing nervously.

LeDuc pulled back down from over the hill to where the others waited.

"Here's the situation: two guards at the front gate with one mean-looking dog." LeDuc looked at Lipp. "You know what to do."

Lipp nodded and removed his rucksack. He reached inside and took out a pouch. From the pouch he removed the stock, prod, and string. Carefully, he began assembling the Barnett crossbow.

LeDuc continued: "Steve—you take out the dog. You get one shot. Make it count. We'll be close enough to take the guards."

LeDuc winked at Valance.

"Once we're inside, Diamonds, we'll sweep through and remove the obstacles. Our primary point of penetration is the elevator shaft. We go down the shaft and get into the vault. That's where Bird comes in and does his thing. You all know the plan. Questions?"

"What about the elevator?" asked Diamonds. "Do you have the combination?"

"We have the combination to the elevator. What we don't have is the combination to the vault. That's known by only two people. They're in the lower level."

"What if they don't talk?" asked Diamonds.

LeDuc leered. "We make them talk."

"Just be sure you get that fucking dog," warned Bingo. "Those suckers can take a man's leg off. And stay downwind. The mastiff has radar for a nose."

LeDuc checked his watch.

"Let's get to it."

Taking the long way around the facility was required in order to keep the wind in their faces. The slightest change in direction could alert the mastiff and warn the guards.

It took nearly thirty minutes for the SEALs to circumnavigate the facility. This route brought them to the parking lot near the front gate. A few cars were parked, apparently belonging to the small staff remaining in Springbok Two.

Lt. Lipp slipped quietly from car to car, staying low and into the stretching shadows formed by the cars from the bright lights along the fence. The surface was concrete, not crushed rock, which lessened the sound of foot scruffs.

When he was approximately thirty meters from the guardhouse, Lipp pulled back on the string, arming the crossbow. Carefully, he slipped a razor-tipped quarrel into the track and locked the arrow into the locking mechanism.

A deadly killing machine, the crossbow was once outlawed by the Church for use in warfare. Yet, by today's standards, the crossbow was overshadowed by more horrendous killing machines, such as the weapon carried by LeDuc, who slipped beside Lipp.

LeDuc carried a 7mm Magnum rifle; the bullets were uranium depleted and could penetrate three inches of steel.

"Take the dog. I'll rock on your roll."

Lipp raised the crossbow, paused a moment to feel the wind, then adjusted.

The bolt shot from the crossbow behind a slight *thump*. Faster than the eye could follow, the bolt pierced the night, finding its mark in the neck of the massive dog.

The razor broadhead tore a perfect groove through

the animal's throat, tearing out the carotid, severing the larynx and snapping the neck.

LeDuc followed with a single shot. The huge silencer muffled the blast.

In the guardhouse, the first guard was hit below the left eye; his body pitched backward and fell in a bloody crumble on the floor.

The second guard jumped to his feet, stared wild-eyed at the dead guard, then started to press a Klaxon alarm.

His hand was extended when LeDuc's second round pierced the heavy plate glass and tore through the guard's chest. His body flew against the door and slid slowly to the floor, leaving a gory trail of blood from the door handle to the floor.

"Let's move," ordered LeDuc.

From the shadows of the cars in the parking lot, the six SEALs, Farnsworth, and Bird moved like shadows fleeing the sun. LeDuc hit the front door of the guardhouse, stepping over the dead mastiff as he entered the room where the two guards lay dead.

Quickly, he studied the electronics panel on the wall. With a swift move he shut off the lights, opened the front gate, and switched off the power to the facility.

The SEALs had cut off the world from Springbok Two.

47

DR. ALICE MERINO FELT GLORIOUS. LYING ON HER bed she felt the warmth of Dr. Hendrik Brand. Their affair had begun almost from the day of her arrival on the project. An arrival keyed to the White Lions' movement. Under orders from her uncle, Colonel Coos van Muerwe, she had carefully recruited Brand, using her beauty and body to draw the scientist into the movement. That was finalized three months before. Since that day she had released her emotions and allowed herself to fall in love with the burly Afrikaner.

The past few days had gone from the initial excitement to one of near boredom; they sat and talked, ate, checked the detonator device as scheduled, and made love at their leisure. Living in a world two hundred feet beneath the surface was like living in outer space. The concept of time was lost.

She quietly slipped out of bed and went to the door of her room. Putting on a robe, she cracked the door and glanced down the narrow hall in both directions.

The guard was probably asleep inside the elevator, she thought.

Stepping into the hallway, she tied the belt on her robe. That was when she stiffened at the movement she felt from behind. She started to turn, but felt a harsh hand close around her mouth.

Staring through wide eyes she saw that the hand was black!

"Keep cool, baby, and you won't get hurt," said the throaty voice of Bingo. His Sykes-Fairbairn knife pressed at her throat.

Down the hall she saw other men appear from inside the elevator. She felt herself moving forward under the force of her captor.

Reaching the opened elevator she nearly fainted at the sight of the two elevator guards lying on the floor. Both had large bullet holes through their skulls.

A man with hard features stepped forward. He motioned to the black man holding her in his viselike grip. The grip released.

"Your name?" asked LeDuc.

Dr. Merino straightened her robe. "Who the bloody hell are you?"

LeDuc placed the barrel of his automatic pistol to her chin. "The man who's going to blow your head off if you don't answer my question. Who are you?"

Dr. Merino blinked once, then said, "Dr. Alice Merino."

LeDuc looked at Bird. The nuclear specialist nodded. "She's one of the scientists who was listed in the report."

"What report?" asked Merino.

Bird answered: "The report provided to my government by your President. He's now a guest in our embassy until this little ruckus is over."

"You're Americans!" she blurted.

"Give the lady a Kewpie doll," said Bingo.

"What are you doing here?" she asked, but seemed to know the answer before LeDuc spoke.

"We're eliminating the threat you've so ingeniously created."

Her eyes went to the vault. "You'll never get inside. If you tamper with what's behind that door you'll turn this facility into a hole deeper than the Kimberly mine."

"In which case you'll die with us." LeDuc leaned into her face. "What's the combination to the vault?"

Before she could say anything, a loud voice boomed from down the hall. "What the bloody hell is going on here?"

Dr. Hendrik Brand stood in his boxer shorts in front of the door of Patricia's room. Before he heard a reply, the fuzziness in his brain cleared fast enough to allow him a quick evaluation of the situation. His mouth agape in fright, Brand started back through the door.

A loud *cough* echoed through the hall. Brand suddenly flipped end over end, crashing through the opened door where he lay half in, half out of his lover's room. Sticking out were both legs. At the ankle of one leg a bloody gore was pooling on the floor.

LeDuc stood with his pistol; a wisp of smoke snaked upward from the silencer's muzzle.

"Bring him here. We need some answers," he ordered Bingo.

Bingo dragged the wounded scientist to the SEAL commander. A grisly trail of blood streaked the floor in his wake. Brand groaned, then shouted in pain as he was dropped in a heap on the floor.

Looking up, Brand had a stream of spittle oozing from his mouth. His eyes darted with that special fear men know when they're wounded, alone, and at the mercy of a cold-blooded killer.

And he made no mistake in his evaluation of LeDuc. A glance at the two dead men in the elevator provided all the assurance he needed.

LeDuc squatted; the pistol dangled lightly as the SEAL rested his elbows on his knees.

"Your President has informed my President that there are several nuclear weapons behind that door programmed to detonate if tampered with. Is that true?"

Brand nodded feebly.

"I've also been informed that you know the combination of the vault, and the means of deactivating the booby trap you've rigged. Is that correct?"

Brand shook his head. "I don't know how to deactivate the detonation device. That was the responsibility of one of my technicians." Brand was showing fright at the coolness, the open cold-bloodedness of his interrogator.

LeDuc looked at Bird. "No matter. We brought our own technician. He'll deactivate the device after you open that vault."

"Don't do it, Hendrik," shouted Patricia.

LeDuc looked at Patricia, then at Hendrik. "Hendrik—that's a helluva name by the way—I don't have time to sit here and socialize. My orders are simple: open that fucking vault and put my man inside. I'm prepared to use explosives if necessary. Of course, we might all turn into a vapor of red mist if that detonates the nuclear weapons. The fall out will be devastating. Your country will be damned near destroyed by the radiation. Not that that will matter to us. We won't be effected. Not by anything. Ever again. Do you get my drift?"

Brand shook his head. "You wouldn't."

"Bollinger. Rig the explosives."

SEAL Brooks Bollinger removed his heavy rucksack and the twelve blocks of plastic explosives. Stripping away the paper cover of adhesive on each block, he began placing the bricks of C-4 at key points on the vault. When finished, he inserted fuses, connected the wiring to the fuses, and ran the wiring down the hall.

Bollinger attached a lead wire to the detonator and nodded at LeDuc.

"Let's get under cover," LeDuc ordered. Then he stopped and looked at the scientists. "Chief, bring these two along. Let's give them a ringside seat for the fireworks display."

"Yes, sir," Diamonds barked. Grabbing Patricia by the elbow, and dragging Brand by the good foot, he hauled the two scientists to the front of the vault.

"Either way," said LeDuc, "you two are history."

Diamonds tied the two scientists together at the vault. Both had a clear view of the explosive packs on the door.

"Count it off, Brooks," LeDuc shouted to Bollinger.

The young SEAL began at ten.

Nine. Brand looked wildly at Patricia, who shook her head.

Eight. Brand squirmed, trying to get to his feet but the pain drove him back to his butt.

Seven. Brand was on his belly, trying again to rise. Patricia kicked him for being a coward and regretted sharing her body with the snake.

"Fuck you!" he hissed. "I don't want to die!"

Six. Brand's voice echoed through the hallway: "I'll open the vault. Please . . . don't kill us. I'll open the vault."

LeDuc winked at Bollinger. The young explosive expert sat grinning, holding the wire for all to see that he had disconnected before beginning his count.

48

COMMANDER BIRD STROLLED CASUALLY INTO THE vault, studied the situation for a moment, then came through the door. LeDuc and the others were waiting the way men do when there's nothing they can offer to the situation. Bird took a pouch that he had carried aboard the helo and went back into the vault.

Silence followed, except for the occasional sound of Bird taking something from the pouch, or a sudden exhalation of air from those waiting.

"I hope he knows what he's doing," said Farnsworth.

"If he don't . . . you'll be the first to know," replied LeDuc, who was putting a pinch of Skoal in his mouth.

"How can you chew that shit?" Farnsworth asked.

"I don't chew. I spit." The SEAL released a long squirt that splashed off Brand's bleeding foot.

In the vault, Bird had the situation under control. The detonator was armed with a trembler switch. Had the vault door been opened by explosives, Springbok Two would now be a deep hole in the earth.

Finding the right wire to disconnect the booby trap was the key. One based solely on that most important element: sheer luck.

And a certain intuition that goes into understanding the minds of people who make such devices.

There were two wires to choose from. One white. One blue.

Cut the wrong wire and the facility would be vaporized. The digital display mounted on the nuclear weapons was lit up with a variety of numbers, codes he expected, designed to lure a meddler into a trap. Change the codes and there would be detonation. Cut the right wire and the current would be short-circuited.

He placed a pair of wire cutters on the white wire. White racists—white wire. He started to cut.

He stopped. *White Lions*.

He recalled seeing the patch of the White Lions on one of the guards. The patch was blue and white.

He cut the blue wire.

Nothing happened.

The sound of the snip resounded through the vault and rang into the hallway.

"I'll be damned," said Farnsworth. "He did it."

The SEALs released a collective sigh. Brand said nothing. Patricia Merino looked wrung out. Her long hair was in her face; on her face was the look of defeat.

"Better send the man the word," Farnsworth told LeDuc.

LeDuc took a small transmitter and extended an antenna. He pressed a red button and the transmitter instantly flashed a radio signal on a preset frequency to a navsat satellite roaming the sky above South Africa.

The satellite transmitted the signal to a receiver on the *Valiant*.

In the CIC, Lord heard the technician say, "Springbok Two has been deactivated."

The first phase of Operation Blood River had been completed.

49

2230.

Major Yuri Demlov was confused by the order
rousting him from a charming poolside conversation with
a svelte blond White Lioness; he was angered by the
order that he found waiting for him from van Muerwe.

"This is highly irregular, Colonel. You want me to
fly a mission tonight?"

"That's correct. I've been informed through chan-
nels that several pilots loyal to the government are planning a dawn air strike on Nagmaal. The aircraft are
located at Hoedspruit. I want you to raid the airfield,
knock out as many aircraft as you can, then return to
base. When they see the power of your Wolfhound,
they'll change their minds."

Demlov shook his head.

"Your money will not be paid until the contract has
been completed. That includes unexpected contingencies. Is that clear, Major?"

Demlov grunted and walked toward the barn.

Twenty-five minutes later the Wolfhound taxied
from the barn and began its roll along the makeshift

runway. Reaching lift-off speed, Demlov felt the aircraft rise into the air. He was about to hit the afterburner when a howling screech echoed through the cockpit.

The signal indicated a heat-seeking missile was tracking on his heat signature.

Demlov pressed the button marked FLARES. Instead of leaving a string of magnesium flares to draw the incoming missile away from his aircraft, the Russian received nothing for his efforts.

In the split second between the Stinger missile making impact with his aircraft and his body disintegrating, Demlov screamed the name of his executioner: "Van Muerwe!"

One mile from the end of the runway, beyond the perimeter of the Nagmaal security forces, in the darkness of the veld, Tragor dropped the empty tube of the Stinger missile he had taken from Boeksa's and watched the Wolfhound explode; two secondary explosions followed as the volatile fuel tanks ignited. The aircraft became a burning meteor racing toward earth.

The report of the explosion on impact was all he needed to know he had succeeded.

Holding the communicator to his mouth, Tragor whispered to van Muerwe, "Meet me at the monument at Blood River in twenty minutes. Bring Loweta and come alone or your daughter dies."

PART SIX:

BLOOD RIVER

50

2400.

THE MOON WAS NOT FULL, BUT BRIGHT ENOUGH TO clarify the ocean and turn the stars overhead into a blinking, twinkling carpet of diamondlike light; a combined light that couldn't compete with the multitude of lights radiating from the deck of the USS *Valiant*. The lights of the flight deck turned the night into day, and while there was enough to impress any of the crew, and allow them to see clear enough to do their job, all would have agreed to the man that the greatest light show in town was the crisp, acetylenelike flames from the engines of the aircraft.

What a sight!

Sitting in the cockpit of his F-18, Sacrette wasn't watching the lights; he was watching the catapult officer.

As were the other pilots locked into the tension of the catapult.

The aircraft waited in low-visibility gray; gray that appeared to gleam. With his head turned, Sacrette saw the cat officer extend two fingers toward the bow and knew the ride was about to begin. Instinctively, he braced himself, then felt the aircraft streak down the launch track. Within seconds he was airborne, his airspeed increasing. He banked right, then pulled back on the stick.

The feel of the aircraft was to his liking; viewing through his "Cat's Eye" lenses mounted on his helmet, he could see clearly out of the cockpit. The Cat's Eyes were new technology, releasing the F-18 pilot from the restriction of night flying by using the FLIR, the forward-looking infrared radar. With the FLIR, the pilot could see on his display what the FLIR picked up; with the Cat's Eyes, the pilot could look out the canopy in any direction and see through all weather.

The new device created a bluish aura in the cockpit, but that was appealing to Sacrette, who looked down to see an F-18 flying onto his wing.

"Welcome aboard, Rhino. You look elegant in blue. Sit tight until the party gets started."

Sacrette saw Rhino wave.

The squadron would group in formation before making the initial run toward South Africa, which was only minutes away.

The F-18 aircraft had been split into two squadrons: Red Wolf would fly tactical cover and intercept while the others with the A-7's would fly strike. This would allow the strike aircraft to fly their mission without worrying about air battles should the SA air force get off the ground. The fighters could handle the SA air force, if there was anything left after the strike.

The primary targets were the air bases; each of the fighters had been designated a certain bombing sortie to escort and protect to and from the target. Refueling would be done from KA-6 Intruders outfitted for air refueling. Once considered the light bomber of the carrier group, the Intruder had been relegated to the supportive role of flying fuel.

Another breed of Intruder, the EA-6A, was designed for electronic countermeasures. These aircraft would be the first to arrive over the target area, utilizing sophisticated electronics countermeasure equipment to "jam" and disrupt the radar of the South African defense forces.

F-14 Tomcats would stand off the coast, protecting the battle group from the deadly Exocet missiles carried by the Mirages should one get through the gauntlet of fighter interceptors.

Other elements of the battle group were preparing for war: the guided missile cruiser *California* was ready with their complement of standoff Tomahawk missiles. With the targets programmed into the memory, the Tomahawk could fire from eight hundred miles at sea and hit a beer can on the curb in Johannesburg—if the beer can was the target. This night there were bigger targets: military installations and key command and control centers of the White Lions and the SA defense forces.

Tough marines were ready to begin an amphibious assault from the LSD *Portland*. From heloes and amphibious assault vehicles, five thousand marines were scheduled to come ashore at key points and provide a stabilizing infantry element and set up a base of operations to return control of the government to the elected party.

At the moment the attack was ready to begin, the aircraft broke off into their designated sortie groups and thundered toward the deck for their low-level approach into South Africa.

In the cockpit of her F-18, Jugs glanced at Gilmore, who was flying off her wing. In a cool and calm voice, she said over the microphone, "Let's go to work."

The hunt was on!

51

PATRICIA GABLE COULD RECALL EXPERIENCING HER
current fear only once in her life; the night her father
was murdered. Sitting beside Tragor, she was silent.
Sensing her fear, he asked, "Do you understand what
you're to do?"

She nodded. "I understand what I'm supposed to
do. What I don't understand is why you're doing this?
Why you're taking this risk. You've gotten what you
came for. Why risk your life for Loweta?"

Tragor studied the young woman. She was dressed
in the clothes worn by Moira Prouse. Her hair was blond,
like the Boer's daughter, and from a distance he believed
she would be convincing. Especially for what he had in
mind.

"I don't know if you'll understand what I'm going
to say. But I'll try to make you understand. For many
years I served my country, rather I served masters of my
country. These masters did terrible things to the Soviet
Union. They will do terrible things again, I fear. Loweta
represents the goodness I once thought I served. I'd like

to give him a chance. In order to do that, I first have to get him back alive."

"And then?"

"Then, I'll let the future of South Africa be decided by whatever course the nation chooses. I would like to stay here, but that's impossible. After all, I am a spy."

She laughed. But only for an instant. Her eyes went to the side of the road, which was flashing by furiously; the road wound through the mountains, often along steep ravines. Patricia didn't look over the edge; she stared straight ahead as the lights appeared to pull the car through the blackness.

"I hope this works," she said softly.

"It'll work."

52

At Nagmaal, Coos van Muerwe ordered one of his soldiers, "Bring the kaffir." Minutes later the handcuffed and gagged Michael Loweta appeared from the massive barn led by several soldiers. The soldiers said nothing, though the situation did appear strange. Noting their suspicion, van Muerwe said, "I'm taking him to Pietermaritzburg. He's going to make a live broadcast."

The soldiers seemed to accept this explanation and wished their leader luck. Van Muerwe drove away, toward the rendezvous.

Overhead, the hum of an aircraft in the distance went without notice.

The only thing that mattered was the rendezvous at Blood River!

53

THE SH-60B HAD SKIMMED THE TREES FROM SPRING-bok Two, dodging hillocks and sheer cliffs until Bird thought he would vomit. When the helo settled on what the pilot figured was the closest site to Nagmaal, the SEALs and Farnsworth dropped out of the helo and began their short jaunt to the road.

Dressed as White Lions, all except Bingo and Farnsworth, the SEALs carried equipment similar to the white supremacists. Nearing the main entrance to Nagmaal, LeDuc halted the formation. "Bingo. You and the chief raise your hands."

The two black men marched in front of the SEALs, their hands held high.

Approaching the gate, LeDuc stepped to the front and spoke in perfect Afrikaans. Diamonds was impressed. LeDuc motioned for the two black men to come forward.

"We found these two kaffirs walking along the bloody road from Pietermaritzburg. We noticed their uniforms are American. I figured the colonel would want to see them."

The guard looked suspiciously at LeDuc. "Where's your vehicle?"

"Bloody rot of luck. Broke down a mile back on the road. Can you get us to the colonel? He'll be anxious to interrogate these two blokes."

The guard shook his head. "He left the camp a while back. Said he had personal business to attend to."

LeDuc gritted his teeth. "What personal business?"

"That's his business, ain't it, mate." The guards were now showing signs of irritation with the new arrivals. "Say, here. Let's see your bloody identity papers."

"Certainly," replied LeDuc. When his hand came up he wasn't gripping papers. He was gripping a pistol. He fired the silenced weapon twice, then watched the two guards pirouette in a tight circle and crash to the ground.

"What now, goddammit! The fucking honcho's gone and taken a hike!" spit Farnsworth. "And watch who you call kaffir!"

"Sorry, Chief." LeDuc thought for a moment. "This is a clusterfuck. Van Muerwe's gone. The air strike is inbound. Let's get back to the helo and check in with Home Plate."

The men disappeared into the darkness and made for the site where the helo was waiting.

LeDuc contacted Lord aboard the *Valiant*. He explained the situation and requested further orders. Receiving the orders, he wasn't certain he had heard correctly. He had the admiral repeat the orders.

After LeDuc broke communications he looked at the pilot and requested his fuel amount. The pilot told him. "That's enough to take a little side tour."

"What kind of side tour?" asked Farnsworth.

"You're going to get to see a lot of Africa before the night's over."

"What do you mean?"

"We're going to Pretoria!"

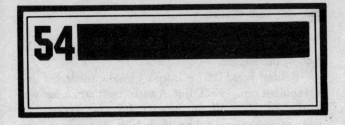

54

1220. Hoedspruit.

APPROACHING THE SOUTH AFRICAN AIR BASE, THE first thoughts of the lead pilot of the EA-6A Intruder were of a Christmas tree. Making his run, he began jamming the early warning radar installations surrounding the air base. Sitting at their radar scopes in the Command Center, the technicians were jerked awake by the unexpected.

Their radar screens were wavy with interference; nothing was clear on the screen except confusion.

Jugs led the first wave into the fight; coming in low, she lined up her primary target with her first Maverick.

A member of the "fire and forget" family of Paveway III "smart" bombs from Hughes, the AGM-65 Maverick has a television camera in the nose of the weapon. Once lock-on is acquired, the weapon is dropped and driven by a solid propellant rocket; guidance to the target is acquired by the television imaging camera in the nose. The weapon can literally be driven through a window; or, in this case, through the front opening of a hangar.

The missile struck with precision, rupturing the shell of the hangar.

Behind Jugs, Lt. j.g. Alissa Gilmore made her first real combat run. The Triple-A antiaircraft attack fire was starting to come off the ground, but she ignored the golden tracers cutting through the sky. At her speed she knew nothing could touch her aircraft. At the release point she punched another Maverick through her primary target: the Command Center.

The bomb went through the air duct on the roof, detonated in the lap of a SA radar technician, and ripped out the top floor of the two-story building.

Close behind, Commander Ed Bines followed with a similar drop, destroying the main floor.

Each pilot had been given a precise target; damage was to be minimized to military targets that could effectuate an immediate threat to the marines coming ashore from the troop ships off the coast.

Noting her second target, Jugs banked hard right, felt her speed jeans light up as the g's increased, then pushed the nose forward. She dropped a five-hundred pound laser-guided bomb through another hangar and watched the structure crumble.

That's when she heard a familiar voice shout over the radio, "Fangs out!"

55

AT ANGELS FIFTEEN, SACRETTE SPOTTED A
Dassault-Bregeut Mirage F-1 streaking along the runway
and scurrying into the sky. Lowering his nose, Sacrette
left the TAC and dove on the Mirage at supersonic
speed.

The Mirage was coming up alone to make a fight.
At this very moment the President of South Africa was
pleading with the air force not to resist. Most listened,
waiting to see who would win in the struggle between
the White Lions and the government.

A few chose to take sides.

The F-1 felt Sacrette tickle him with his APG-65
radar, seeking lock-up. This forced the F-1 into a defensive posture, the worst thing that can happen in an
air battle. The F-1 buried its nose, losing its own radar-
sensing capability, trying to elude Sacrette, who stayed
on the F-1 with tight, inside bat-turns as the Mirage tried
to get around behind Sacrette.

The next move by the F-1 was a climbing maneuver,
taking the Hornet to pure vertical; at the peak of the

climb, the Mirage nosed back to inverted and split the S, trying to shake the veteran American fighter pilot.

Sacrette stayed with him, locking him up again with his radar. The signal was screaming in the F-1's cockpit. The pilot could do nothing but try to evade.

"Come on, son," Sacrette whispered to the pilot of the Mirage. "I admire your courage, but you know you're outgunned and outmatched. Give it up."

The Mirage turned another tight circle and pulled his nose up, flying level with Sacrette.

The CAG saw the Mirage closing; Sacrette banked hard right, then kicked left rudder. The instinct saved him from a stream of 30mm cannon fire, and allowed him to bat-turn onto the Mirage's six o'clock tail section.

On the HUD, Sacrette watched the targeting box turn to a circle, and pressed the firing switch.

An AIM 9L Sidewinder missile shot from the right wingtip missile fairing, cut a red streak through the sky while tracking the Mirage.

Seconds later impact was made at the Mirage's single jet engine. A ball of flame erupted; a split second later, Sacrette saw another roar of flame as the cockpit disengaged and the seat rockets lifted the ejection seat into the sky.

The seat rode straight up, hung for a moment, tilted forward, and began an acute angle of sink as the canopy began to deploy.

Through the bluish tint of his NVG's, he saw the pilot sitting in the saddle of the parachute harness, waving his fist at Sacrette as the CAG streaked by close enough to kiss the pilot.

56

Van Muerwe stood where Piet Retief's believers had been revenged: Blood River. Where Pretorius's column slew the Zulus. Where his heritage was carved into the souls of the children who would follow.

Children. His thoughts were with his child. Not the White Lions movement. That would sustain itself. Tonight he came to the place of redemption for the man who would dare steal his child and trade her for an airplane.

The vilest of thoughts.

He was waiting by the marker with Loweta, who had a rope around his neck. He was still handcuffed, tape covered his mouth.

"Do you hear the sound, kaffir?" asked van Muerwe. "Listen. You'll hear the battle cry of the Afrikaner. 'Retief's plea,' some call it."

There was only the mournful sound of the wind winding through the valley, twisting along this place where brave people had fought for what they believed belonged to them as a birthright, and those who believed they owned title through the hand of God.

The next sound was the stirring of the bush as feet moved across the ground. Van Muerwe heard the sound, and pulled Michael Loweta to his knees with a sharp jerk on the rope.

The moon was dim, but the Afrikaner saw two figures approaching through the darkness. The figure in the rear was taller; the one in front shorter.

"Moira," van Muerwe whispered. He could see her uniform shining off the moonlight. Behind her walked another person. The man he knew was her kidnapper.

Tragor stopped out of range of van Muerwe. "Have you been listening to the radio?" the Russian asked.

"What radio?"

"The radio airwaves are filled with the excitement. The United States has come to assist the government in overthrowing your revolution."

"That's a lie." Suddenly van Muerwe realized he didn't have his radio.

Tragor held up the radio communicator he took from Roos. "Here. Contact Nagmaal." He pitched the radio to van Muerwe.

As the Afrikaner's hands went up to catch the radio, his thoughts were momentarily severed from his daughter, who stood only close enough to barely see. His fingers closed around the communicator, and as he gained control of the device, and pressed the button to make contact, he heard a loud roar.

Then he felt his body flying backward. He crashed to the ground, looking through tearing eyes as his fading senses tried to give him his last few messages.

He saw the blond hair approaching through the darkness. Felt the warmth of the body pressing close to him, smelled the soft scent of her body.

"Moira. My lioness." He tried to pull her closer, but there was no strength in his arms.

He could only lay there and listen to the radio, to the chatter from hysterical voices at Nagmaal.

The command center was under attack.

Nagmaal was in flames.

The White Lions were dying, and with their death, Retief's Vision was dying.

Coos van Muerwe looked up to the tall man standing over him with a smoking pistol. He thought to swear at the man, but chose instead to say, "Don't harm my daughter."

"I won't," said Tragor.

With that, Colonel Coos van Muerwe, a man raised to believe that he was to lead his countrymen to safety, died thinking he had saved a daughter who was already dead.

57

LT. J.G. ALISSA GILMORE CAME IN LOW, LINING UP ON the largest structure on the grounds. Triple-A was streaking up, creating a panoply of golden light; she ignored the fire, concentrating on the target. If she was hit, she was hit. Otherwise, she would deliver the package as planned.

Pulling up at the right moment, she released a "smart" bomb, watching the FLIR as the laser-guided bomb arced toward the target. Impact was followed by a thunderous clap she couldn't hear or feel, but she could see the target disappear in a cloud of fire which was like a white light against the FLIR.

In a matter of minutes, the strikers had reduced the secondary target to nothing but rubble. As a wave of marine assault heloes approached, the defenders of Nagmaal, the White Lions, had had all they could handle.

As squads of tough young American marines assaulted the defensive positions of the farm, they met little resistance. The air suppression had killed, maimed, bombed into submission the men and women who sought to tear a nation apart in order to form a more perfect nation. A nation never destined to bear fruition.

In the distance, Tragor, Patricia, and Loweta stood by the memorial at Blood River.

The light from the bombings was unmistakable; the roar of the heloes resounding; the taste of victory succulent.

"Did you know about this?" Patricia asked Tragor.

The Russian smiled. "Yes. Boeska received a message from one of my operatives in Durban yesterday morning. The Soviet military was tracking the American battle group moving onto the coast of South Africa. It was a calculated maneuver on the part of the Americans. It may or may not prove to their advantage."

"Advantage. That's your world, isn't it?" She was suddenly angry. She had seen too many results from the game of political "advantage." None of which she liked.

"It's the only world I know. It's a world you could never understand." He walked off toward van Muerwe's car.

"Where are you going?" she called to him.

Tragor turned for a moment. He studied the lovely, brave young woman standing in the pale African moonlight. He wanted to say many things. Instead, he said, "Take Mr. Loweta to a safe place. Take Boeska's car. I'll take van Muerwe's car. You'll both be safe if you use your heads and don't draw attention to yourselves."

Tragor climbed into van Muerwe's car and started the engine.

"Will I ever see you again?" Patricia cried out.

Tragor didn't reply; he drove away, leaving a white woman and a black man standing alone on the birthplace of the Afrikaner state.

The future was theirs to decide.

58

THE SEAHAWK SH-60B CUT A SMOOTH SWATH THROUGH
the air above Pretoria; below, the lights of the city were
nearly darkened. The targets had been hit. Farnsworth had followed the reports of the air battle over the
headset as he rode to the capital from Springbok Two.

"Pretoria's a heaven 'n' hell city, Diamonds," said
Breaker LeDuc. "A bit of heaven . . . a lot of hell."

"Yeah," Farnsworth said softly. He looked off to
the distance and saw the faint fires glowing from what
he suspected was a township, where black Africans were
venting their rage at the government that was neither
standing nor fallen. A government in midflight.

Up or down? Time would tell.

"What are you thinking, Diamonds?" asked LeDuc.

The CPO grumped, then said, "For all its problems,
there's no place like the good ol' U.S. of A. God Almighty. I can't imagine living in a place where I couldn't
be treated like a man."

LeDuc said nothing. He slid back against the web-
bing of the seat and watched the city pass by.

A few minutes later the helo began its descent onto the roof of a building. The American flag was flying from the staff at the top of the roof.

Diamonds watched the flag, mesmerized by the colors as the helo glided to a landing.

When the rotors settled, Diamonds stepped from the helo. A squad of embassy marines approached, wearing battle utilities and carrying their weapons at port arms.

LeDuc stepped forward, took a salute from the young lieutenant commanding the squad, then asked, "Where's the President?"

A door opened and the President of South Africa strode forward, followed by the U.S. Ambassador to South Africa. Both men looked tired, worn to the bone.

Diamonds saluted the President, then the ambassador.

The President walked to the helo, paused at the door, acting as though he wanted to say something to Farnsworth. He finally turned and climbed into the helo.

Farnsworth saluted the ambassador and then went to the helo.

The ride was uncomfortable for Diamonds. He sat next to a man he hated in principle, a man who represented the most oppressive country in the world where Diamonds's race was concerned.

Then he thought about the situation: The man was trying to change the situation. If he hadn't been trying, van Muerwe wouldn't have had a leg to stand on.

After a long silence, the President turned to Farnsworth. He extended his hand and said, "Thank you."

That was all he said. Nothing more.

Diamonds didn't need more. He watched the land

below; the city turned to veldt, open country, then the Drakensbergs. Somewhere below there was a whole nation of people trying to be a nation within another nation of people.

Then he smiled, and then grinned; finally he released that long, throaty Farnsworth laugh, and reminded himself: *God . . . tonight I ran in the footsteps of the Zulu!*

And he found comfort in that thought.

Battle Damage Assessment

0530.

JUGS WAS SITTING AT HER DESK WHEN SACRETTE came into her office. Lt. j.g. Gilmore was sleeping in a chair. She was still wearing her flight suit and speed jeans. Jugs looked tired, but she was doing what she always did after a flight, whether in combat or training. She was filling out the performance sheets.

"How about a drink?" Sacrette asked unceremoniously. He held up a bottle of Aberlour scotch.

She put down her pen and reached to the drawer. As her hand came out with two Styrofoam cups, she seemed to freeze. She looked at the CAG. "You've never invited me for a drink before."

" 'Times they are a-changing,' or so the song goes." He sat on the edge of her desk and poured until the scotch nearly spilled over the top.

Sacrette raised the cup and toasted, "To navy carrier pilots . . . the best of the best."

"Aye, aye, Skipper." She took a deep drink, then lowered the cup to her desk.

Sacrette drained the cup in one blast and was recharging when she asked, "What's the problem?"

Sacrette looked at Gilmore and shook his head; he seemed to envy how the kid had flown her first combat strike mission and could now sleep like a baby. "After my first mission, I couldn't sleep for three days."

"That was different."

"Why?" he asked.

"You knew you had to do it again. She knows she'll probably never fly in combat again. She's had her ride of a lifetime. And she survived. Hit all her targets. Dead level center."

"Maybe we better keep her. It would be a shame to lose good talent."

Jugs stared at Sacrette for a moment, then looked away quickly, the way women do when they suspect a man isn't being honest.

"Is there something you'd like to tell me?" she asked.

He nodded. "The targets are taken care of on the ground. The marines are establishing control points. The President of South Africa has issued a plea for the military to stand down. It's working. As a matter of fact, most of the white South Africans are rising up against the White Lions. I suspect in a few days the situation will be stabilized."

"Business as usual?"

"I don't think so. New business." He poured another drink.

"Tell me something, Boulton . . ."

He realized it was the first time she had ever called him by his first name.

She continued: "Are you trying to write me one of those terrible letters?"

Sacrette's head dipped slightly, then he whispered, "Yes."

"Is it Ed?"

"Yes."

"Is he down?"

"He's dead. His aircraft was reported lost en route back to the carrier. Sea AIR Rescue couldn't find anything." Sacrette stood and walked out of her office.

Jugs stared at her paperwork, then at Alissa.

She thought about Ed, and the pain. More importantly, she thought about the pain of writing a letter to Alissa's parents. Then she recalled the young woman's bombing run, coming in low, hugging the deck, laying the package right down the slot.

For the first time in a long while she respected Ed Bines. For all his faults, he had taught the kid well, as he had taught her.

He was gone, but he left something behind: damned good pilots!

A former paratrooper and combat veteran of Vietnam, Tom Willard holds a commercial pilot's license and has lived in Zimbabwe and the Middle East.

﷽ HarperPaperbacks *By Mail*

NIGHT STALKERS by *Duncan Long*. TF160, an elite helicopter corps, is sent into the Caribbean to settle a sizzling private war.

NIGHT STALKERS— SHINING PATH by *Duncan Long*. The Night Stalkers help the struggling Peruvian government protect itself from terrorist attacks until America's Vice President is captured by the guerillas and all diplomatic tables are turned.

NIGHT STALKERS— GRIM REAPER by *Duncan Long*. This time TF160 must search the dead-cold Antarctic for a renegade nuclear submarine.

NIGHT STALKERS— DESERT WIND by *Duncan Long*. The hot sands of the Sahara blow red with centuries of blood. Night Stalkers are assigned to transport a prince safely across the terrorist-teeming hell.

TROPHY by *Julian Jay Savarin*. Hand-picked pilots. A futuristic fighter plane. A searing thriller about the ultimate airborne confrontation.

STRIKE FIGHTERS— SUDDEN FURY by *Tom Willard* The Strike Fighters fly on the cutting edge of a desperate global mission—a searing military race to stop a fireball of terror.

STRIKE FIGHTERS—BOLD FORAGER by *Tom Willard*. Sacrette and his Strike Fighters battle for freedom in this heart-pounding, modern-day adventure.

STRIKE FIGHTERS: WAR CHARIOT by *Tom Willard*. Commander Sacrette finds himself deep in a bottomless pit of international death and destruction. Players in the world-wide game of terrorism emerge, using fear, shock and sex as weapons.